# Tales From The Milleran Cluster

## The Journey of Awri

### Kenneth P. Langer

**Brass Bell Books and Games**

BRASS BELL
BOOKS & GAMES

# Contents

# Chapter One

## *Letter To My Granddaughter*

Everything you know is a lie. All that you have been told is false. All the things you have come to know about him: his life, his journey, even his words were distortions of what really happened to him. Yet, he was still a great man. He deserves to be remembered. He deserves to be honored because he inspired many after him to do great things in his name.

Maybe I shouldn't say these things to you, my dear. You are precious to me and I want your memories to be good ones. After your mother died and you came to live with us, we worked hard to erase the old memories and build new ones, happier ones, but now I am threatening to change that. How can I? I only consider the idea because I feel that though the truth may be uncomfortable, in the longer view of things you will be better served by it. There is always more to be seen in the full light of day.

You know the story.

But, no. Maybe you don't. His work is banned, after all. Most copies of his works have been destroyed and the few that remain are secreted away in dark inaccessible places. Yet, the story persists. It is told from one to another in whispers or in rooms far away from the passing crowds. It is the guiding light for the Torans, a beacon in the dark against the silent but pervasive oppression of the Corps, a bold revision of the whispers of the Dreamweaver.

Sometimes a secret is more well known than the published edicts of the Grand Council especially when that secret contradicts the Council's idea of history and propriety. I assume that everyone knows the story of Ishlan and eir journey to Kugoya as it has been told to us by eir first proselyte Awrithrich Eight or "Awri." It has become a legend of epic proportions and, if you believe the propaganda of the Council, it has been the source of conflict and revolt, especially in the North. But the Council has been effective in its efforts.

Maybe you don't know. And maybe you shouldn't.

The Grand Council of Corps of Pa'Kevutu have brought together the people of the islands and the mainland. They have helped to develop a way of life that is both grand and comfortable. They have given the people of these lands purpose and function. We have lived in relative peace and prosperity but those luxuries come at a price: imposed conformity. At some point we each have to consider whether contentment dictated by the limited confines of the Corps is better than the sloppy and erratic discomfort of living free. Which would you choose? There are many who prefer the former. It is easier. The parameters of good living are clearly defined. It is the well-lit path but it is restrictive. There is no chance for deviation, for exploration. All other paths are forbidden.

Is this the path you wish to walk, my granddaughter?

I am cognizant of the irony here. You have discovered this small work of mine hidden away in the folds of your pack. You may have been preparing your bunk and your space in the academy dormitory and maybe it slipped out onto the hard floor. You opened its pages and read my words in the midst of one of the very Corps that have helped to enforce the ways of the Council.

You chose to become a recruit of the Wesuran Security Corp and we made no attempts to stop you. We know you have to follow your own heart and that you are guided by good intentions. You want to help others, to offer them protection, to be a leader among the people. How could we fault you for that? Besides, we were once there ourselves when it was known as the Savuran Security Corp. But that was before the evolution of Toranism, before the Journey of Ishlan, before the Chronicles were written.

Of course, the choice is yours. We have raised you to be independent and strong and you have always exceeded our expectations. You have pursued your own interests with zeal and passion. I expect nothing different now. All I want is that you know the truth so you will not enter blind into any commitments.

But, before I begin, let us go over the source of all the fervor: the story of Ishlan. Like all well-crafted fabrications it contains kernels of truth and moments of captivating beauty. It is worth a hearing if for no other reason than it is both enlightening and entertaining.

So, here. I offer you both stories: the fabled journey of Ishlan as described by eir follower Awri and the journey of Awri himself as best as I can recall. They are, for the most part, both a story of one person but in many guises.

Awri was a friend, a trusted companion, a seeker of truth, a follower of passion, an inspiration, and a fabricator of falsehoods. Most importantly, though, he was a person who followed his own heart against all odds and made it easier for others to do the same.

If nothing else, the reading will help you pass the time between the challenges you will soon face at the academy: those prescribed by your new life/work entity and those imposed on you through your own personal convictions. I hope it helps but, whatever you do, don't let them see you read it.

# *Chapter Two*

## *The Nature of the Universe*

### From The Chronicles Of Enlightenment

*Editor's Note: This manuscript by the one known as the Revealer is a description of the universe as a manifestation of the geometric image of the torus. It was first discovered on Keshon after he vanquished the mysterious onset of illness that plagued that island.*

The universe. It seems so still and quiet, so vast and nebulous. We stare up into it on dark evenings. It is spread out across our eyes in every direction like an enormous veil held above us. It is a shroud of black pierced with pinpricks of dancing light. Those stars in the firmament flicker and twinkle like children playing on an empty beach.

We lie there, heads nestled in the golden grass and stare up into the night. The ground holds us firmly in its grasp as we look into the silent depths. We perceive no motion, no sound, no centrality. Yet, our eyes and ears deceive us. We are lulled into a quiet comfort amidst the embrace of the night sky but the fires above us rage in a tempest that is far from peaceful and cozy.

The universe is not still and quiet. It rages and fumes; it is in constant motion. All that we believe that is still is forever in flux. Even the ground we lie upon travels. Every moment evolves into the next; nothing remains still forever. Even we ourselves are never the same from one moment to the next.

How do I know this? Have I traveled between the stars? No, but I have seen their nature. I have seen the motion of the universe in one image. I have talked to the angels who have seen it. They showed it to me. I will tell you so that you may know the truth.

The universe is a hurricane, a violent swirl of power, a spiraling cacophony of endless transformation. It is our home and in its midst we are able to sit silently and ponder its essence but we are fooled by the passage of time. Change happens at different rates, some so imperceptible we barely notice, but the change is there nonetheless. There is change amidst change within more change. Each progression moves in its own time.

The universe is a cornucopia of nested vortices. But that is only how it appears. That is its surface, its face, but not its totality. Beneath the surface, beyond the seen, is another vortex spinning away from the first. Together, the seen and the unseen combine to create a complete unity.

These two entities fulfill each other, inform each other, define each other. Together they form one whole, one unified reality–perfection. Together they form the great double vortex that sustains itself.

Together they make the Torus.

# Chapter Three

## *The Death of Ishlan*

### Pa'kevutu: The Island Of Kugoya

I think back now to that day and I wonder how I did not see it: the beginning of the end for someone I thought I knew. The truth is that we never really know anyone–least of all ourselves. We present an illusion, an amalgamation of images we think others want to see. We constantly work on how we should look rather than focus on our own true nature.

Detective Shorixuvich Twelve "Shorix" was like that. He worked to please others, to become what they thought he should be. Don't get me wrong, he was a good detective. He could have been a great detective but he gave it all up that day. He was no longer the Shorix I knew. He became something else, someone else. He became a person no one could have expected.

It happened the day the Shadow-Keepers left the small world of Pa-Kevutu, the beginning of an endless stream of deceptions.

Despite what you may have heard, the Shadow-Keepers were not a band of evil beings intent on doing us harm. They were the first people. They tried to protect us from ourselves but no one understood that. When they were discovered they were hunted down like criminals. They made the island of Kugoya their home and there they were pursued by the secret Wesandt Protection Corp. Wesandt pursued them for yerons and finally discovered their base on Kugoya and there they decided to destroy them once and for all.

Why? The soldiers and the Ceorans they worked for said they

wanted the Shadow-Keepers' advanced technology. The Keepers were able to move themselves about the mainland and the islands of Pa'Kevutu with relative ease. No one was sure how they did it. It was said they interfered with our children, that they were responsible for the Third Child Syndrome. What really made them objects of disdain and pursuit were the stories of how they attacked other Corps and stole important research and materials. I don't think any of those things were the real worry of the Ceorans who ran the Corps, though. I believe it was that there were others not in their control and that to them that was unacceptable.

We tried to stop them because we knew who the Shadow-Keepers were. We knew what would happen, what did happen after they were gone. They warned us of the consequences of over-population and the depletion of resources. They tried to tell us about the danger of developing technology without considering the consequences. No one listened; no one believed them. The people of Pa'Kevutu were sure the land was theirs to do with as they wished. It was a foolish assumption with delayed but dire results.

We took a stand. We decided to fight for the Shadow-Keepers. We decided to resist the fear and ignorance that makes people alienate and attack one another. Shorix paid a heavy price for that effort but not as much as did the one we knew as Izzie.

You see, before E was known as Ishlan the great prophet of Kugoya and the founder of the people of Toranism, E was Izzie, the false and doubting Parak priest. But, no one tells you that.

Izzie called emself a priest, an abrasan, but admitted that E had never taken the final vows required of the clergy of the corp-created religion of conformity known as Parakonism. E had misgivings about the religion. E saw the contradiction of dictating to the people of Pa'Kevutu the proper ways of being good workers and Citrans while ignoring the needs of the unfortunate and the itinerant.

E joined us in our efforts to defend the Shadow-Keepers and was mortally wounded. It was in eir final moments that E saw his purpose in life. E took what E learned from the Shadow-

Keepers and combined it with eir own spiritual insight. In that last moment E was no longer afraid of death.

"I want you to know that I'm not afraid," E said to us that day.

We knew then that we had lost em. I wanted to run and get em some help but, in reality, there was little anyone could have done for em. I chose to stay and listen to em. Maybe it was the wrong choice. Maybe I could have found some improbable way to help em. I don't know but E insisted I listen to eir words. E wanted eir thoughts to live on even if eir body would no longer carry them.

"I thought Perfection was the sacred goal of every Kevutian," E said. E was referring, of course, to the idea that every Citran of Pa'Kevutu had an obligation to seek perfection. It was an old idea, one that used to mean something completely different from what the Corps and their contrived Parak theology created. Perfection, as defined by the Grand Council of Ceorans, is found in being a good employee and a model member of a society under the control of the corps for which you work.

"I thought it was what made life worth living," Izzie continued. "But I was wrong."

That was when I noticed the first crack in the foundation that had been my wopar or work partner Shorix. A seed of doubt was planted in him but it was of no delicate flower or blooming vine. It was the germination of a weed that grew and spread with tenacity.

Izzie spoke of the legend of the Dance of Death and explained how it was a distorted story and a metaphor for the energy of the Dance of Life and the vortex–the secret to their power. As if swallowed by a wall of ice the face of my friend Shorix grew stiff and cold. He had seen the great swirling waters at the center of Kugoya and was moved by their beauty and ferocity. Izzie saw that enormous whirlpool too but, to him, it was a symbol of the meaning of death. As he would say: the end of one vortex is but the beginning of another.

Through pain and stiffness, Izzie whispered, "Death is where Perfection is found, not life. Life defines death and culminates at its point. I do not fear it. I shall become Perfection. I shall join the source of all beauty and love which is that Perfection."

Shorix never said another word that day or for many days to come. I, too, was touched by Izzie's words and sought for some way to comfort em, to honor em for eir insight. I took the hand of the one we knew as Kozan Izzie and proclaimed em Ishlan, the Prophet of Kugoya. The newly named Ishlan then died before us and, though chaos surrounded us on all sides, we heard nothing but the dread of silence and felt the horror of stillness.

I thought that was simply the sad end of a chapter on the lives of people lost to the follies of arrogance and intolerance.

I was so wrong, so terribly wrong.

# *Chapter Four*

## *The Face of Destiny*

From The Chronicles Of Enlightenment

*Editor's Note: Before the Revealer became the interpreter of revelations from the Prophet, he encountered the mysteries of the Shadow-Keepers who occupied the island of Kugoya until their demise. It was part of the mythology at the time that the Shadow-Keepers were responsible for the maintenance of the environment of Pa'Kevutu and that this feat was accomplished by the maintenance of an enormous swirling pool of seawater. Through his encounter with the Shadow-Keepers (whom he calls angels) the Revealer became aware of his destiny.*

Once I was shown the beauty of the vortex I wanted nothing more than to be a part of it. I wanted to dive in and be pulled into the dance of dances, the Dance of Life. It was so simple and in that simplicity was the immense beauty of it all. Like a moment of silence that breaks into the hustle and bustle of life, the drab clamor that fills every moment of every night and every day in the capital city of Yakrutich, the sudden absence is numbing. The heart embraces the fleeting moment of peace and is refreshed. Or, like the sip of cold water that is found in the midst of the searing heat of a day in the south of the mainland, the thirst is quenched and the spirit is lifted. That was how I felt looking into the center of the world.

Below me the water whirled. The sea rushed in and fell upon itself. It began as a great circle then twisted into a point so far below and so tight I could hardly see it. There it disappeared. And there, too, I wanted to go–to disappear, to become no more a part of the madness of life, no more to be pushed about by unseen forces, no more to run in circles with no worthy destination. No more. I wanted to dive straight into the emptiness at the center and be pulled into it.

In my mind I lept. I spread my arms and let the wind catch me on my way down to the center of everything. The walls of water rose up to embrace me. My body turned and tossed into the great flow of energy that formed the central whirlpool. I felt no fear, no remorse, only peace. My heart let go all its anxious yearnings. The roar of the water became a voice that welcomed me to the essence of all reality. I was pulled into the center until all became darkness and silence.

There I floated, something that was and was not, something in the midst of time and space itself. I was all things; I was no thing at all. I was in a place everyone knows but no one remembers. It was the center of something with no center. It was the beginning and ending of reality. It was the ground of all being. It was without substance, without meaning, without purpose yet was essential to all of these things and more. It was Paradise.

Then it was revealed to me that this paradise was the birthplace of all things. All of humanity came from Paradise. From there developed the first world. All the people came from this first world. This was the world of the angels–the Angels of Paradise.

All this I saw at the water's edge. All this was revealed to me and I felt fulfilled, completed. What else was there to know? What else was there to do? There could be nothing more. When one has seen the core of all that is, when one has felt the presence of all life, when one has known the simple truth that is the center of all things known and unknown, there can be no more to experience. The beginning of life is also its end.

My life reached its culmination in that moment. There was no more reason to go on. I wanted to die in that truth. I wanted to run into its arms and let it embrace me. I wanted to die and, in so doing, be reborn into the beauty and wonder of this infinite mystery.

I knew my life was over–the life I had once known. I could not imagine another so I committed myself to ending the journey. I would send my body where my mind had gone. I would join the angels.

But they would not allow it. They spoke to me and I heard them.
"What is it you seek?" they asked.
"Answers," I said.
"Do you know the questions?"
"No, but I know the answers lie before me," I said.
"That is so."
"If I know the answers then the questions will also be revealed."

"That is also so."

I took a breath and stared out into the abyss. "Then I only seek to understand the nature of that which is before me."

One of the angels emerged from the rest and came to me. "It is a symbol of the ever-changing reality," the angel said. "There is no beginning, no ending, there is only the evolving."

"Then that is the answer," I whispered.
"It is," the angels responded in chorus.
"There is no need for questions. I seek to be no more. My life is complete."
"Yes," said the one angel before me. "One life is complete but you are more than one life. Your next life is just beginning."
"Next life?"
"You are Awrithrich of Eight, the Revealer. You are the messenger of the angels. You will hear our words and carry our message to the people. That is your life now."

And with those words I understood my purpose. I accepted my destiny and committed myself to fulfilling it. I stepped away from the water and turned back to the land. I walked, without destination, without guidance, without fear. I just walked until my path was clear.

# Chapter Five

## On The Move

Pa'kevutu: Kugoya    The Northern Beach

M ay you die well and proud so that you may rise up to kiss the stars," I said to the figure of the one who we named Ishlan.

Eir body slumped into the ground. There was a restful silence, a long-awaited peacefulness that settled over eir frame. It was like everything E had ever sought in life was granted to em in death. All E had ever wanted, all E had ever talked about was being a priest, an abrasan, a genderless angel of Perfection, so that E could help others find their own peace. E never took the vows, though, so E was not able to work among the people E loved.

It was a futile dream anyway and E knew it. Parakonism was the sovereign domain of the Corps. It was their way of making control and obedience more than just an employee's obligation. Their laws became a moral and spiritual covenant. Being a good employee became a sacred journey toward Perfection—a perfection defined by the masters, the Ceorans of the Corps. The Ceorans banded together and formed the Grand Council to codify their principles of obedience. E could never rectify eir sense of fairness with the Council's rules.

So, E pretended to be an abrasan while E did eir best to avoid the minions of the Council. E became an itinerant rogue priest but E was never able to do what E wanted. It was not until the moment E let go of eir own life that E felt free to express eir thoughts and ideas. And, E did. E claimed that death was the culmination of life, the point at which all the meaning of a lifetime is put into focus and from that clarity we achieve the Perfection we seek. It was a shocking message, I agree, but I had no idea how much it would affect my partner and, through him, the rest of the world.

Shorix was already shaken from meeting the Shadow-Keepers. He saw how they controlled the environment of all of Pa'Kevutu. Somehow their parting words sent him into some kind of out-of-control fall. His entire jovial light-hearted personality disappeared. When I turned to look at him, I saw his face but no one was there.

"Shorix!" I said. He said nothing. I put my hand on his back. "Shorix," I repeated. "Are you OK?" He didn't move. His warm breath formed into silky clouds before him.

The Shadow-Keepers rose into the sky in a ship like none of us had ever seen before. It was not a vessel of the sea but a ship of the sun. It rose above us, striking fear and awe into the hearts of all who saw it, then it extended a sail across the sunlight and drifted away into the depths of myth and perplexity. The soldiers and bullies who became the Wesuran Security Corp called that moment the Day of Reclamation. Cheers and jeers were heard all around us as the grunts made their way across the island. We were not their heroes. We tried to stop them.

"Shorix," I said again. "We can't stay here. We have to take Ishlan and move. They'll find us soon."

As I said those words the shadow of a figure overtook us. I reached for the knife at my side but stopped when I recognized the face. I knew her as Kim, someone who helped us challenge the original Wesandt Security Corp and defend the Shadow-Keepers.

"What are you two doing?" said Kim.

Uekimoy Three or "Kim," as she was known, was obstinate and crass but she was an excellent fighter. At one time she was part of the very security Corp we fought against but she came to see the true intention of her boss. He wanted to kill the Shadow-Keepers. He wanted what they had. He wanted to know what they knew. He orchestrated the raid of their island and enlisted the help of everyone who had ever had any dealings with Shadow-Keepers.

Kim had been one of those. She was an obedient employee of

Wesandt until she was sent on a secret mission to investigate the Shadow-Keepers. She was caught and when the Keepers explained what was happening, she saw the truth. She wanted to help defend them and was mad at being deceived by her former employers. The mix of zeal and anger made for a deadly combination.

I turned to look at Kim but said nothing. Instead I moved aside until the body of Izzie was revealed in shards of light.

"Oh," was all she said. There was hardly an inflection in the expression of that one word but I knew that, for her, it was the most emotional expression she could muster. Kim looked at Shorix then back at me. Shorix barely moved, his face was blank. I shrugged.

"You can't stay here," Kim said.

"I know," I replied. "But I've got a dead abrasan and the empty frame of a Detective I used to know here."

"OK, which one do you want?"

"I'll take stone-face," I said grabbing Shorix by the collar.

Kim picked up the priest from the floor and tossed em over her shoulder with a grunt. When we got back out into the open, some of our other buddies joined us and we worked to get out of harm's way. Shorix reluctantly came along but the noise and confusion sparked something in him. He stopped.

"Now what?" Kim said.

"Higher!" Shorix called out.

"What's he talking about?" Kim puffed.

Shorix looked into the sky. "Higher," he shouted again.

"Is he crazy? He wants to go up? There's nowhere to go."

Shorix turned his eyes to me for a moment as he said, "Hier!"

"He doesn't mean 'higher' as in up," I said. "He means "Hier," the leader of the Shadow-Keepers." I turned to face the dazed man and shook him as I talked. "He's gone. Hier is gone. They're all gone."

He looked at me. I thought maybe I had broken through and found a connection with the partner I once knew but there was nothing I recognized in that gaze. He wasn't looking at me, he was looking through me, as if he could see the truth hidden behind my eyes, as if he could see into my very essence. Then, he ripped himself away from my grip and headed back into the chaos of the open countryside. He was a decent fighter but he had no chance against the professional combat force of the Wesandt Corp.

I was unsure of what to do. The look that he had bore into my soul took away my senses. Kim looked at me and I must have appeared curious because she cursed out loud and tossed the body of the abrasan into my arms before she turned and took off toward Shorix. She caught up to the man, tackled him, and then popped him across the face with a single blow. He went limp. Kim slung him over her shoulder and dragged him back to the group.

"Can we please get out of here now?" Kim asked. People were taking notice.

"Yes," was all I could say.

I had no energy to come up with some kind of clever comment on the situation. I just wanted to get away and try to figure things out.

# Chapter Six

## *The Attack of the Demons*

From The Chronicles Of Enlightenment

*Editor's Note: This manuscript references the eviction of the Shadow-Keepers from Kugoya by the emerging Wesuran Security Corp. Thinking that the Shadow-Keepers were the angels of Paradise, the soon-to-be Revealer fought to maintain their grip on the lives of all Kevutians. After encountering the Prophet he came to understand the importance of independence.*

And so I walked. I walked through the jungles and the towns, along the rivers and the beaches. I walked until I could walk no more. Then I came upon the open sea. There the waves repeated the words of the angels into my ears. My life's purpose, my destiny was to convey the story of the life of the Prophet, of the Blessed One, and of the message they sought to bring to the world.

I stared into that forever horizon until the skies grew dark and the seas became angry. Clouds developed from light skies and filled the space above me. They darkened the sunlight and turned day into premature night. They grew from small innocuous puffs of cream-colored wonders into enormous rolling fiery embers, sentinels of a storm.

The seas rose and churned spitting white foam and spray across the beaches. Water slapped into rocks and sand and from the midst of those waves came the demons.

They came for the angels. They came for the Prophet and the Blessed One. They came for me. They poured onto the land in waves of destruction. They tried to silence us. They tried to hold on to the lies of the past and blot out the truth.

But we fought them back.

When they could not defeat us by force they tried to confuse us through deception. They spread confusion and lies until we were nearly turned against each other but we remained strong, solid in our faith of righteousness.

Yet they managed to injure our revered prophet.

I speak of myself as if I am of any significance. I am not. I am merely the storyteller, the presenter of revelations. Ishlan, the Prophet of Kugoya, is the story. E is the reason for the narrative and the hope. E is the spark of the fire that warms the heart. E is the flash of light that illuminates the path. E is the warmth of the hand that we hold for comfort on the journey. E came from the shadows and was gone too soon.

This is what little I know of em. E began life as a simple farmer. There E learned to love the land. E learned to grow things. E planted the seeds and blessed the soil. E raised the crops and spread eir bounty to others.

But there came a time when it was not enough. E helped the plants grow and E helped others eat and thrive but that no longer fulfilled em. When E walked the fields, the stones spoke to em. When E led water to eir crops or felt it fall from the sky and nurture the plants, E heard the raindrops call to em. When the winds blew and made eir stalks dance and sway, E heard their whispers. All these things beseeched em to search eir heart. This E did and realized that E could do more, E could help more people.

E learned the teachings of others. E heard the words of the Crusoms and the Zulos and was taught in the ways of the Paraks. E was trained in the manner of the Kozans. E studied to be an abrasan so that E could help others wear away their burdens and sorrows. E chose to become one of them. E strove to take their vows but never did.

The Prophet never took the vows because E met The Blessed One. She put doubt into his mind and made him consider other possibilities. She brought em out of the shadows and into the light. She guided em, she protected em until E was ready to reveal the truth to the world but it was not her words that led em on the sacred path. It was the vision of the waters of the vortex–the same one I had seen. The same one that had so moved me.

E knew that E would soon be taken by the angels. E knew that his ending would be the beginning. The truth was revealed to em and through em to us. When E was delivered, eir life became complete, eir mission fulfilled. Thus began the era of the Torans.

# Chapter Seven

## *The Emergence of Awri*

Pa'kevutu: The Northern Forest Of Kwanchu

N ot that way," I whispered.

The unconscious body of Shorix was strewn across Kim's shoulder with his head pointed toward the base of the tallest mountain in a range of peaks. The relative center of the island of Kugoya is surrounded by a series of mountains and the highest is Mount Polisum. It was a logical destination. It was far from the beach and would offer spectacular views of the entire island. If I was a Shadow-Keeper that's where I would have based my operations.

"Why not?" Kim said, turning around. She didn't look happy with having her decision contradicted.

We headed South, away from the beach and into some thick woods. It was the best move to get out of sight.

"Because that's where everyone is headed," I said.

"OK, Chief Detective, which way?"

"That way," I said, pointing Southeast. "Along the tree line for cover then out to the beach at night."

"The beach?" wailed Kim. She lowered the inert body of Shorix onto the a floor of leaves, sand, and soft dirt. She realized her mistake and stopped herself. This was not the time to attract attention. "It's too risky," she said in a softer tone. "Even in the dark."

"I'm betting we still have some friends out there and we need all the friends we can get."

"The Thalysto?

"Yeah."

Kim reached down to grab the man on the ground and grunted out an "OK" as she did.

I walked past her with the dead body still on my shoulder and we moved as quietly as we could through the dense brush and forest.

I think we were close to our destination. The central range of mountains peaked through the treetops directly to our South. Shorix started groaning. We ignored him at first because the sounds coming from his throat were few and soft but they grew in intensity and frequency. To make things worse, he was squirming and his sounds became louder.

I turned to Kim and said, "You'd better put him down."

"I guess I didn't hit him hard enough," Kim said as she lowered the abrasan onto a mossy root that curved gently from a tree and into the ground. She propped his head against the tree and did her best to make him comfortable. She stared into the man's face. "He's coming around."

I put the figure down onto the dirt and took the chance to work out the knots and pains that had set into my upper body. Next, I walked over to the side of Shorix and knelt down.

"How is he?" I asked.

"Dazed. Confused. You know, he's his usual self."

I looked at Kim and opened my mouth to say something when Shorix let out a loud groan and rocked his head from side to side. Then his eyes flew open.

"Whe… Where am I?" he asked, staring into empty space.

"Kugoya," I answered.

"Kugoya," he whispered in return. His eyes drifted and searched the woods as if he might find something to confirm what I said. Instead his attention landed on the dead body on the forest floor. "The Prophet," he whispered in reverence.

"Shorix," I said. He didn't move. He didn't even flinch at the sound of his own name. "Shorix," I repeated but with no result. I placed my hand on his and he responded with a flinch. His eyes drifted down toward my hand. After he scrutinized my hand, a glimmer of recognition twinkled in his eyes and he looked at me.

"Exi?" he asked, as if I were someone he had just run into at an academy reunion.

"Yeah, it's me," I said.

"Exi!" he repeated with the hint of a smile on his lips.

I removed my hand from his and settled myself into the ground. "I've been worried about you, partner. What happened?"

His lips curled up a little at the ends of his mouth. "You don't need to worry about me, Exi."

"It's just you haven't been acting yourself lately," I said.

"Yeah, buddy," added Kim. "Snap out of it. We need you."

Shorix moved his head toward Kim then back to me. "That's the thing," he said. "I haven't been myself my whole life. I've been living a lie and now that lie has been exposed. Now I will be who I am."

"And who is that?" I asked.

"Awrithrich," he said. "Awrithrich Eight of the line of the Prophet."

"A-what-what?" Kim blurted.

The former Shorix pivoted his head toward Kim. "Awrithrich Eight," he said again.

"And where's the first seven?" Kim asked.

"The eight is symbolic, not representative," he said. "It stands for the four directions and the four corners of all space. It is the number of Sacred Sisters in the sky…"

"There's only seven…" Kim interrupted but Exi stopped her.

The man once known as Shorix continued. "It is the first cube of even numbers, a symbol of Perfection created through the union of opposites in three dimensions such as…"

A twig snapped and Kim thrust her hand over the man's mouth. We withdrew our knives from their hilts and prepared for action. More pops and snaps followed and it soon became clear that a patrol was passing nearby. We had no idea of their intention. Mag, the Ceoran of Wesuran promised to stand down after the Shadow-Keepers left. He announced plans to turn the island into a research center but both Kim and Exi knew he could not be trusted. We embarrassed him in challenging him and blocking his objective. He was the kind to take that insult personally and find a way to even the score.

The patrol moved on without incident.

"We've got to keep moving," Kim said softly.

"OK." responded Exi. "Let's make sure they are gone and then we'll head out."

"No," blurted Awri.

Exi moved toward the man. "Shorix, we've..."

"Awri," he said.

"OK, Awri. We have to move..."

"No," said Awri. "I have to tell you what happened. I have to tell you right now, this moment. I have to tell you about my father."

# Chapter Eight

## *The Dance of Life*

From The Chronicles Of Enlightenment

*Editor's Note: This manuscript is a description of a famous practice used by many Torans as a form of ritual.*

But let us not grieve. Let us not stand still and weep while the world turns and rolls on its merry way. Let our minds be still while hands rise in adoration and praise. Let the body be lifted and rise into the motion of the stars.

Dance and sing!

Dance because it makes you feel good. Sing because you hear the inner music. Celebrate because you can. Movement is the desire to express the rhythms of the body. It is how we play in the winds of change. The weeds in the water maintain their place by flowing with and not against the tussling of the waves. The Besher flower does not grasp the sea but spreads its petals and floats along its undulating surface.

Thus we are released from the illusion of stillness. We become part of the rollicking and romping that is the movement of the cosmos. Dance and sing not as a distraction but because it is the essential movement of all things. Escape the falsehood of stature and permanence. By the time you have stood still long enough to stake your claim there will be nothing left to grasp and no one to hear you.

We stand still and proclaim our significance but we are nothing more than waves upon the sea. We rise and we fall and it is the motion that is significant for it creates the flow of all life. Release yourself and become part of the flowing waters. Rise and fall in the seas and winds. Spread your arms to catch the breezes and dance in the song of the mountains.

We form a circle to dance and sing like all things at all times. We are a model of the universe. We are an homage to the vortex. Turn the circle and move your bodies. Feel the rhythms, join together. Spin as one. Unite the mind, the body, and the heart together as a single being. Bring yourself into a joining of the many. Hands together we spin and turn, moving about a center that is not fixed.

We come together, hand-in-hand, to form the circle of life. We encompass the center of the world. Where is the center of the world? It is wherever we focus our attention. All places are the center for there are no edges to a circle.

So it is with the self. The center is the focus of attention. There are no edges to attention. The center is where the heart is, not the heart of blood and air but the heart of the self, the heart where body and mind unite. Here the circle of the self spirals in and then returns. This is the flow of the world. This is the flow of love and joy.

So we dance in the flow and, by so doing, enact the dance of the universe. We dance in the dance of all things. We dance the Dance of Life. We are the dance and when we move we join with all things.

# Chapter Nine

## *Seekers of the Dance*

Pa'kevutu: The Island Of Kugoya

H e was a journalist," Awri began.

Kim rolled her eyes then sat on the ground in resignation. She let out a sigh.

"You must have been very proud of him," I said. I moved closer and tried to comfort him.

Awri's eyes looked up and into the distance. They darted back and forth as if searching for something. His mouth hung open in an expression that was filled with both wonder and fear. It was as if he was watching a story unfold before his eyes, a story that had only now come together and was in danger of breaking apart and disappearing.

"I... I don't remember that part of my father's life but I do recall that he talked about his experiences. He was proud to report the events of the day to his people, at least until those events became tragic," Awri said.

"What happened?" I asked.

"The Resistance of the Western Islands."

"The what?"

"They don't teach that one in the Detective Division of the Wesuran Academy, I'm sure," Kim said after a laugh. "When the Grand Council was in its infancy in Kevutu, it was decided that it should extend its control beyond just the mainland and include the Corps of all the islands. Not everyone liked the idea, especially the Corps of the Western islands who were far from the mainland. The Council took action and the methods they used to bring the

Western islands into the fold where, shall we say, more than suggestive and less than humane."

"He was born on Kerich and could understand why the people of that small island did not want to be controlled by bullies from the mainland," Awri said. "He grew up a pacifist. He detested violence. He thought that by being a reporter he could help keep the peace but nothing could stop the advance of the foot soldiers of the Council."

"There wouldn't have been much he could have done," Kim added. "They would have rushed in unannounced and taken over. Their first objective would have been to control the flow of information. The journalists would have been detained before lunch. Your father would either have been fired or trained to become a megaphone for the Council and their policies."

"Do you remember any of that?" I asked Awri.

"No," he said.

"What do you remember?"

"Her death. His death."

"Your mother and your father?"

"Yes," said Awri. My mother died first. She worked in the Finance Division. There was an attempted robbery. She was killed," said Awri. He paused, then continued. " My father was devastated. He loved her beyond measure. Then things turned upside-down."

"What do you mean?" I asked. Even Kim became interested and turned her head to listen.

"I don't know," Awri began. "My father flipped, became someone else."

Kim scowled at me but neither of us said anything about the irony of the situation.

"Go on," I said.

Awri sighed. "He became angry, hateful. He blamed his neighbors and the people of his island for delaying the implementation of the Council. He claimed that if they had acted faster, a security corp could have been in place and the robbery would have been thwarted. He moved us all to Kevutu and joined

Savuran."

"Guess he didn't stay a pacifist too long," Kim said.

Awri made no response.

"That must have been hard for you," I said.

Still no response.

Kim rose to her feet using her hands to push herself up from her knees. "OK. So what?" she said. "You had a rough go of it. Everyone has troubles in their childhood."

"He killed himself," Awri said without a hint of emotion.

*Oh my dear girl I remember that moment so well. It was like the whole world ceased. We heard absolutely nothing. The leaves on the trees stopped moving and the wind froze in place. I don't even recall breathing. But, let me return to the story...*

Awri closed his eyes and continued. "He couldn't reconcile the differences: pacifism, anger, revenge, love, loss, pain. It all became too much to bear."

Kim and I listened. What could we say?

"His Commander came to us one day," said Awri. "He said we would be taken care of. Said our father had done good work. Said his life was a model of Perfection for others. His name would be added to the Garden of Remembrance. Though I was devastated by his death I was never more proud of him."

Awri fell silent while Kim and I stared at the ground.

Kim said, "I don't understand. How does the death of some wanna-be priest change anything?"

Awri remained silent but I spoke. "It's what the abrasan said before he died that changed everything." I looked at the man slumped by the tree. "Shor... I mean Awri believed the words of the corps when they told him his father had died a hero, not a coward. I'm guessing he joined Savuran himself as a way to maintain his father's memory and his image.

He was told his father's death had meaning insofar as it demonstrated his commitment to the Corp." I looked to Awri for confirmation but got nothing, so I went on. "But Ishlan changed all that. E said Perfection was found in death and not life. That meant that life, in and of itself, has no meaning. Only the choices we make are significant and defining." I looked again at the figure of Awri slumped forward. I looked at Kim and saw she was beginning to understand. I did not want to have to explain any further and hoped Awri would speak his own conclusions.

"Well, um... Awri," said Kim. "That about right?"

Nearly buried between his arms, Awri's head nodded.

"What will you do now?" I asked. I think maybe it was a mistake to ask him that so soon. Maybe he wasn't ready to think. I'm not sure, but the moment came and went. The wheels of destiny were already in motion.

Awri lifted his head. "To prevent others from making the same mistake."

"You mean to keep other people from committing suicide?"

I flashed Kim an angry look for her insensitivity but she was unfazed. Apparently, so was Awri. He continued without a change in his voice or position. He was past all the emotional upheaval now. He had already committed to the next step.

"There are many ways to end your life. Some do it physically and end their pain but others do it emotionally, or mentally. Their bodies may remain alive but other parts of them are walled off and killed. If there is no growth, no experience, there is no living. Ishlan offered us ways to see beyond the stagnation. I want to help others live through his vision."

I thought about what Awri said but was not sure what he had in mind, what he was planning. I tried to find out by walking toward him while I reached out to him. "Awri, look, I know you're hurting right now and that everything is a little confusing but..."

"Seekers of the Dance," Awri said.

I stopped moving. "What?"

"We are all Seekers of the Dance of Perfection. All life dances. We are but steps in the dance. Hear the music, feel the motion, be swept up in the reverie."

Awri looked off into nothingness but when I moved closer to him he looked right into my eyes. "Fellow Seeker," he said with a firm tone. "I wish to be alone."

I moved my mouth to speak but was stunned. He did not use my name. I was no one in particular to him anymore. He wanted little to do with me. I could not help him anymore.

"OK, OK," I said. I stepped back and moved away.

# Chapter Ten

## The Blessed One

From The Chronicles Of Enlightenment

*Editor's Note: In this manuscript the Revealer discusses his call to sea and his encounter with someone he called The Blessed One. There is some speculation as to who this person was but nothing definitive has come to light. Whoever she was, we know she was responsible for much of what we have learned of the Revealer and his writings.*

Water. It is the lifeblood of all things living and not. It is both soft and hard. It cannot be grasped yet it can sweep away entire land masses. It falls on a hot day and quenches the thirst of people and plants yet it can also pull them down and drown them. It is steam and mist and it is ice and frost and we see it gathered in the mighty sea.

The sea speaks to us. It contains the voices of all things in its waves. It sings all songs and whispers all secrets.

I was called by the sea.

I heard its whispers. It spoke to me so I found a ship and boarded it. I knew not where it was bound nor the length of the journey. It did not matter. It was on that ship that I met the Blessed One.

Let me tell you of the Blessed One.

She was exalted by the angels at her very birth. She was the third of three children at a time when it was only possible to bring two into the world. She was a Third Child—a rare and divine thing. The third child born of any family was once condemned to an early death but the Blessed One was brought into the world and protected by the angels. They taught her the secrets of the vortex so she could tell others. She was spared so she could deliver to me her message. We found each other on that journey through the waters of the future and I heard her words.

She taught me about Paradise. She taught me that all things, all people, all life came from Paradise. Paradise was the land of the angels who were sent out into all the worlds to bring life to them. There they began new towns and cities where the people could grow and thrive. They taught them their ways. They showed them the dance.

They came to this world and did the same but they were not accepted. They were feared and shunned. They were chased and hunted. They took refuge in the center island and did their best to continue to help and protect the very people who scorned them. They did their best to maintain the peace and prosperity they brought to us. They came to bring us light but were relegated to the darkness. They hid and did their work where eyes could not see them. They became the Angels of Kugoya known to the people as the Shadow-Keepers.

Eventually they were hunted down. They flew back to Paradise and to the peace and beauty they had tried to bring to us. Now our world suffers. We cannot bring them back. We know not where Paradise may be. We cannot go there.

Of the Shadow-Keepers we know not their origin. They come from eternity and offer us wisdom. Yet, they are so beyond us that we cannot comprehend them. We do not understand their ways and, so, we confuse their actions of righteousness as displays of arrogance and are threatened.

We must not depend on them to save us. We must find the circle ourselves and draw up our own center. We must become our own angels. We must seek the perfect society in the same way that we must seek the perfect self for the one and the many are the same. Both are part of the same Perfection.

The many make it possible for the one to pursue Perfection and the one leads the way for the many.

# *Chapter Eleven*

## *A Sailor's Tale*

### Pa'Kevutu: The Sea of Islands

The grizzly old man slammed his mug down hard onto the wooden table in the midst of a storm of raucous laughter.

"Did I notice him?" he repeated, then laughed even louder. He threw his head back into the air as if he needed more room for his ear-pounding cackling to break through his chest. Above him a lamp swung from side to side.

"Did I notice him?" He wailed for a third time. "How could I not notice him? He was a thin scrawny thing. I could tell he hadn't ever sailed anything more than a toy boat in his tub. He turned green the minute he set foot on the deck."

I remembered the last time I saw the former Shorix on a ship. It was a challenge for him to walk up and down the wide deck and try to keep any food in his stomach. He eventually...

"Got the hang of it," the old man said, finishing my thought. "Not that he had him much choice. Ya either get better or ya shrivel up like bad fruit and die. He didn't die." The rusty disheveled old sailor took a big slurp of ale from his mug. "Maybe he should have," he added.

"Why's that?" I asked.

The sailor wiped his sleeve across his mouth but it was more an act of delay and distraction than it was an attempt at some kind of orderliness. "Terrible sailor, that one." He set his mug down. "Nearly got himself killed... more than once." He leaned closer to me from across the table so that I could smell the ale fester in his mouth and dribble down his unkempt beard. "First rule of the sea, Detective." He smiled but revealed more empty space than teeth. "Don't die."

"How did he die?" I asked.

The old man moved his mug aside and brought his hands together. "First couple a times was just stupid. Didn't know what a jibe was."

I knew enough about sailing to know the inherent danger in the maneuver called a jibe. "Let me guess, he…"

"Wham!" yelled the cantankerous sailor. He slapped his hand against his forehead. "Went right down, he did. Blood everywhere. Think he was lucky, though. His skinny body offered little resistance to that swinging boom. He went flying across the deck like he had been shot from a catapult. Did a pretty little twirl on the wet deck then folded up against the hull like a sack of dirty clothes."

The sailor reached for his mug again and lifted it to his lips. He let his head fall back until the cup was completely inverted. He lifted the mug and looked at it in surprise. Nothing but a few drops fell from it. He slammed it down on the table.

"The second time," the sailor continued. "He nearly got himself tossed into the sea for all times. Ya know, ya gotta be careful walking the deck. There's a lot of ropes and crates. If you're not careful you can get your foot caught on a line and then find yourself hangin' by your toenails and kissing the sea swells."

There was a dark twinkle in his eye I had seen too many times in too many people. "He just tripped, did he?" I asked.

The sailor shot me a quick smile and a short laugh but added nothing.

"I imagine he wasn't too popular with the crew," I said.

The seaman offered another laugh but nothing else.

"And the third?" I asked.

The sailor lifted a spindly etched finger and tapped it against the lip of his empty mug. I sighed. I didn't want to have to serve as his personal barkeep but, for the moment, I needed him. I stood up from the tiny table, grabbed his filthy mug, and moved toward a keg.

We were sitting in a small room in the midst of a ship at sea. The room was where the sailors ate their meals but also served as a kind of rec. room between meals. I filled his mug with a smelly frothy substance that flowed from the keg and then returned to the table.

After Awri disappeared from the woods we went looking for him but more patrols were added every minute we stayed out there. We had to give up and clear out. Just before the last rays of the sun crawled over the horizon and into the dark sea, we saw what we had been looking for. In the distance we could make out the sails of the Thalysto, a beautiful though battle worn carrack that brought us to this island in the first place.

The ship looked beautiful to me with her high fore and aft decks, two proud square sails, a triangular foresail, and her two dwarfed waving topsails that beckoned us to come aboard. The ship was too far out to swim to so we took a chance by making a fire signal. Her captain, Niona, sailed into shore then came up to the beach in a rowboat. Her relatively new friend, a scraggly old fellow we called Captain Milos, and one of the few Kevutians to have actually spent time with the Shadow-Keepers rowed. Niona stood behind the bow sporting a loaded coilgun in each hand. She was taking no chances.

"Didn't think I'd see you two again," Captain Niona said in a crackled voice.

She helped us into the rowboat and took us back to her ship. When I explained what happened with Shorix and how I wanted to find him, they agreed to help.

The Thalysto was a cargo ship and Niona made her limited fortune moving materials around the islands but she was well compensated (some might say over-compensated) for the journey to Kugoya. Could she have retired comfortably on some isolated beach for well-off Citrans? Sure, but the sea was her life and she wasn't leaving it. Besides, her and Milos seemed to tolerate each other.

We sailed all along the northern coast of Kugoya avoiding the

Savuran ships. We explored any other ship that took aboard a ranting apostle of a strange religious tradition. I knew it was the most likely way Awri had found to get off the island. Whatever he was searching for was somewhere else and the only way to get off that island was on a sailing vessel (unless, of course, you were a Shadow-Keeper).

This sorrowful excuse of a sailor now before me had been one of many sea scum I interviewed on those different ships. The difference was that this sailor had actually seen Awri. The disciple had been on their craft.

"The third what?" the sailor said.

"The third time he nearly got killed," I said.

The gruff old man slurped on his ale and held his cup in his hand.

"Right," he said. "That." He put his cup down then straightened himself in his chair. He looked me in the eyes. "He hit an officer."

"What?"

"Not sure what really happened. He may have just bumped into him. Maybe he provoked him. No one knew. No one cared. We wanted him gone, is all. Something was bound to happen. Just a matter of time."

"Then what happened?" I asked.

"The officer ordered the others to hold him. He was going to clobber him good himself. The officer picked up something wooden and walked over ready to beat the guy to death."

"Were you there? Did you see this?"

"Yeah. I was there. Saw it all. The officer had that wood raised high toward the skinny guy when suddenly the officer stops moving. It's like he just couldn't move anymore. He just stared back at the guy."

"Awri?"

"Yeah. That's what he called himself. They say he just called out a name and the officer stopped. Turns out he said the name of the officer's father. They say he started talking about how hurting others doesn't help with your own pain or something like that. Anyway, the officer dropped the club and walks away. Craziest thing I ever seen. That's when things really got weird."

"What do you mean?" I asked.

"Well your guy starts talking to the crew. It's like he can see right down into your soul. He feels the pain you're feeling. He tells us to become who we were meant to be and other such crazy talk."

The sailor turned away. He lifted his cup to his lips but stopped in thought.

"Sounds like he had quite an effect on the crew." I said.

"Yeah. The captain nearly tossed him off into the drink. Said he was disrupting the order of things on his ship. The crew defended him though and things calmed down. Suddenly no one hated the guy anymore."

"Did you ever talk to him?"

Yeah, once."

"What did he say?"

The sailor put his mug back down and looked at the table. "I didn't understand most of it. Something about connecting to something greater than ourselves but first we had to connect with ourselves, then others, then everything and when we did we walked the Path of Perfection. I don't know. Something like that. I told him if he spouted that stuff on land anywhere he would be locked up in some crazy house."

"And did you believe it?" I asked him.

The sailor lifted his head and stared straight into me. "Look, I'm just talking to you because the Captain said so. Said you were some detective from the mainland or something. Had to answer your questions."

I knew not to push him. "So where did he go?" I asked him.

"Funny thing. We were headed to Keshon for supplies when a ship from there flagged us. They said there was some kind of sickness or something on Keshon. Half their crew got sick before they could set sail. Warned us not to go there. The Captain turned us about right away."

"What's so funny about that?"

"It was the last time we saw that Awri guy."

"He disappeared?"

"Some say a few of the crew got him on a boat headed for Keshon."

"Keshon?"

The old sailor looked at me again. "Is that guy crazy or what?"

"I don't know," I said. "I just don't know."

# Chapter Twelve

## *She Dreamed a World of Paradise*

From The Chronicles Of Enlightenment

*Editor's Note: This manuscript was found among a collection of poems and notes most of which were incomplete or unreadable. At first glance the work appears to be an artistic break from the philosophical discourses of the other manuscripts but it may be early evidence for works to come. The Revealer's language becomes increasingly challenging and confusing as his life and pursuit of the ultimate truth continued. These rhymes may have been an attempt to maintain order through rhyme in a rapidly changing mind. Whether these changes were due to mental instability or the attempt of a mere human to comprehend the spiritual mysteries of life is difficult to know. This particular poem presents the beginning of the work of the Blessed One.*

In a time before time,
Before the raging sea,
Before the howling winds of change
Brought all that was to be,

A sacred woman of pure heart
Greater than the open sky
Grew weary of unfettered life
But knew not how to die.

Of one thing she was certain:
That not all was what it seemed
There was, oh, so much more
When she closed her eyes and dreamed.

She envisioned the winds and water.
She dreamed the rocky shore.

She saw the light of sunshine
Reveal the forms of more.

She spread her arms out wide
And breathed into the wind.
She set the stars in motion
To make them swirl and spin.

She blew the whirling winds
And sent them west and east
She stretched them north and south
Until the gyre increased.

And from those wisps of starlight
Came all the things we know:
All that we see and touch,
And all that shall live and grow.

She dreamed a world of Paradise
And the angels that filled its lands
Then she chose one among them
To bless with her own hands.

She cast the angels to the stars
To find her child a home.
Thus she sent the Blessed One
And to us she was shown.

But the once sacred purpose
To which she was embossed
Became entangled in the weaving
And to her will was lost.

She grew up among the people
And suffered as they would
Until the toils and trials developed
A compassion true and good.

As she walked among us
And grew in empathy
She came to know the truth
And learned her destiny.

# Chapter Thirteen

## A Plague of Misfortune

Pa'kevutu: The Island Of Keshon

O h Sacred Sisters!" Kim muttered under her breath. We both struggled to be silent, to not let the entire scene before us throw us into hysterics. I was trying to stay still and breathe. What we beheld was horrific. There was row upon row of hastily constructed beds each with a person struggling for life. The lucky ones were sleeping. The rest filled our ears with moans and groans. Bodies writhed and turned in their makeshift cots. Fluids from bottles and bags hung over the people with lines that drained into their arms. The less sick of them strode back and forth between the debilitated. They bent down and said things. They tried to smile. Some administered medication or changed sheets or fluids. The air was thick with the smells of sickness: waste, medicine, sweat, vomit. Mostly it contained the clouded odor of fear.

"Excuse me," I said. I tried to get the attention of one of the helpers but he ignored me. Attention fell only to those in the beds. If you weren't horizontal you weren't noticed.

"Forget it," Kim said. "They're not going to talk to us. They've got more important things to do."

"I suppose you're right. Let's see if we can find someone in charge." I led Kim out of that room and we looked for someone who might be in charge of this chaotic nightmare.

I recalled the scene from the day before. I ended my interview with the merchant ship sailor by pouring him yet another mug of ale. He waved me off and probably fell asleep. The Thalysto had been near the merchant ship the entire time so all I had to do was take the small boat I used to get there and row myself back. After I got back on board we set sail for Keshon. I told Kim and the others what the sailor said about a sickness on the island but we were not prepared for what we saw when we got there.

Kim and I went from room to room and saw the same scene: people in pain and struggled and others tried to help them. We were ignored by all, but in a distant room we saw a woman standing over a stack of papers.

"Excuse me," I said.

The woman did not look up at us. She flipped through the papers, snapping each page as she turned them over. She clearly was not happy with whatever she saw.

"I'm sorry to bother you but we're looking for someone," I said.

The woman snapped the top page of her papers back into place and then gave us a look of fire and anger. "Everybody's looking for somebody here." She put the stack of papers on a nearby table with a solid pound of her palm. "Now, as you can see, I have a lot to do here and I don't have time to talk to you. If you're not on a bed or hovered over a bed then you're in the way. Now, if you'll excuse me..."

The woman was not in any kind of uniform but wore a standard kevan and let the bottom half swirl around and brush against us as she went by.

"His name is Sho..." Kim started to say.

"Awri," I broke in. "His name is Awri."

For a moment I thought I had made a grave mistake. The room went eerily quiet. I wondered if Awri had angered these people just like he had first done with the sailors. I was prepared for the worst.

The woman turned on her heels and came at me in a hurry. I thought she was going to punch me right there in the hallway. I saw Kim in the corner of my eye slide closer to protect me. Instead of attacking me, however, the woman grabbed my collar.

"Awri? Have you seen him?" she said in desperate high-pitched voice.

"That's what I came here to ask you."

"I'm sorry," she said, letting me go. It's just that, well, we need him."

"I don't understand," I said.

The woman walked over to the open entranceway of one of the room filled with cots and languishing patients. We followed her.

"He just showed up one day. We were in the midst of this terrible sickness. Some have called it a plague. He started to help out. At first he did what the other volunteers did. He changed sheets, checked medications, held people's hands, then he started talking to the patients. I don't know what he said to them but he comforted them with his words. He had a certain way about him. He had a kind of aura. I can't explain it but people felt better whenever he came around."

"What have they got?" Kim asked.

"That's just it. We don't know. It seemed to come on all of a sudden."

"You a doctor?" I asked.

"Just got out of the academy. I'm a little out of my league here but we're short handed."

"When did it start?" Kim asked.

"Just a few days before he got here." The doctor said then she turned to us. "You know he asked me those same exact questions."

"He was once a detective," I said wistfully. "What was he doing before he disappeared?"

"Asking a lot of questions, interviewing the patients, checking blood levels. I thought maybe he was a doctor as well but when I asked him about it he said no. When I asked him what he was doing he said nothing. Just kept asking more questions."

"What sort of questions?" I asked.

"Same kind of stuff: when did it start, how long has it been going on, what kind of symptoms did they have, that sort of thing." The doctor stopped and took a step closer to us. "Then he said something very strange to me. He said it wasn't a plague and it wasn't a disease."

"Did he say what it was?" asked Kim.

"No, he didn't say anything else. That's when he disappeared."

"When was this?" I said.

"A day or two ago. I'm not sure. It's hard to keep track of time in here."

I was baffled. He must have come here to help but then stumbled onto something. I nodded toward the patients. "Do you mind if I have a look?"

"You a doctor?" the woman said with some hesitation.

"No," I responded. "I was once a detective myself, back in Yakrutich. I saw a lot of things in those yerons. Maybe I might recognize something."

"Like he did?" Kim muttered.

"Maybe."

"Well," said the doctor. "I guess it couldn't hurt." She walked us into the room and past the rows of cots.

"What are their symptoms?" I asked.

"Aches and pains, mostly in their joints, some have numbness and a loss of coordination, others are just unusually exhausted. Some have a strange pallor to them."

"What do you mean?" I asked.

She didn't answer but, instead, walked toward one of the cots.

"How are you today, Yavo?" she said as she sat down beside a patient.

The woman turned her head and smiled when she saw the doctor. She was probably middle-aged but looked much older in her condition. She was covered in a white sheet. Her hair was strewn around her head and her face looked drawn and tired.

"Much better now that they gave me some medicine," the woman named Yavo said.

While the woman responded, the doctor reached under the sheet and withdrew the woman's hand. The doctor placed her own hand atop the woman's hand and tapped it gently as she talked.

"Well, you get some rest now, OK?"

The doctor kept tapping the woman's hand. It was a sign and I followed it. I compared the hand of the patient with the doctor's. They were not the same. The hand protruding from the bedsheet was darker. It had an eerie smoky-gray coloring.

"Yavo," I said, coming around to the other side of the bed. "Do you mind if I ask you some questions?"

"Well," Yavo said looking at the doctor. The woman holding her hand nodded in response.,"I guess so."

"When did your symptoms start?" I asked.

"Well, a while ago, I guess," Yavo said. "Started having some pains. Then stomach cramps. Got so I didn't want to eat much. But I didn't want to lose my job. Just got it a while ago."

"The corps don't look kindly on sick pay," Kim muttered.

"Where do you work?" I asked, ignoring my colleague.

"This new plant they put in."

"Doing what?"

"Not sure, really. Makin' some kind of solar thing."

The doctor put the woman's hand back under the sheet then turned to us. "After the resistance movement in the Western Islands, the Grand Council focused their attention on those islands for expansion and industrialization. We were mostly a pleasant place to stop along the way. Then the Council turned their attention to us and the Island of Kejawi. They started building factories and digging mines to build solar cells that could power some kind of ship they were working on.

"Did it ever occur to you," I said. "That this sickness and those plants may be connected?"

"Well, no," said the doctor. "The representatives of the Council told us they were perfectly safe. We are not part of the Western Chain. We were happy to get new Corps here to help provide for us. They took care of us. Why would they want to harm our people?"

"The harm may not have been intended but the consequences were certainly ignored," I said.

"What are you saying?" the doctor said with alarm.

"I'm saying that I think our friend Awri may have been right," I said turning my head to look at all the people on the cots. I stepped away from Yavo so she would not hear me. The doctor followed.

"This is not a disease. I've seen these symptoms before. It looks like lead poisoning."

"Lead poisoning?" the doctor repeated. "But, how?"

"Those factories," Kim interjected. "Your patient said they were working on solar cell parts. Those solar cells are made with methylammonium lead halide. If not handled properly the lead can be mixed in the air with dust or with food or water. It can take a long time for the symptoms to manifest if ingested slowly over time."

I looked at Kim. I knew she was smart but she seemed all too familiar with something the Corps would have tried to keep secret.

"How do you know this?" I asked Kim.

"You forget who I used to work for," she said.

"If you're right," said the doctor, "we can find ways to treat it. But that won't help you find..."

There was an explosion, a heavy one by the sound of it but it wasn't close enough to damage the clinic. It was close enough, though, to rattle the windows and make everyone sit up and pay attention.

"What was that?" the doctor gasped but I was already moving before she finished the question. I grabbed Kim by the sleeve and took her along until she ran with me.

"Where are we going?" Kim asked.

"To go get him before he does anything else," I said.

# Chapter Fourteen

## *The Land of the True Self*

From The Chronicles Of Enlightenment

*Editor's Note: Much of this manuscript is believed to be damaged though some have speculated the author may have been, instead, writing the work in fragments.*

So the Blessed One was born and taken by the angels. They raised her and taught her the truth. And because she was not inflicted with the curse of the Third Child and because her heart was pure she became blessed.

She was raised without knowing...

...was guided by the search for truth. She became a seeker of truth until the conventional existence could no longer support her. She became...

... lifted by the hand of one...

...she sought but could not be found.

But because she wanted to know more about her origins she took to the sea. There she and the Prophet were brought together.

Influenced by their teaching but unaware of their actual influence...

...into the very heart of the Prophet. Though confusion was already...

...like the brilliance of a thousand suns.

It was the Blessed One who first caused him to entertain a different way of looking at the things. She taught him to consider things beyond the purview of the corps.

The vision of the vortex became clear. In it he became aware of the essential...

...became the sound of his calling.

Thus The Enlightened One, the Prophet, was sent into the Land of Emptiness to discover the Inner Self. There the truth was found, the beginning revealed, and the prophecy begun. The path to salvation begins with throwing off the cloak of convention and beginning anew with the stark reality of the true self–whatever that may be. Only then can one's true purpose be known.

The Prophet was directed to Kugoya to dwell in the house of the angels. There the great storms and tempestuous winds were calmed so that he could enter into their sanctuary but the demons had sent them away. The seas were stilled and he came unto the shore. He entered the battle of the demons and in a moment of brave conviction he stood his ground in the name of truth and...

... struck down. In that moment of impending death he was faced with the pureness of truth. In that moment and in that place the world was changed forever. It was there that a single enlightened person became the one we we know as Ishlan, the Prophet of Kugoya,

There the Prophet learned of eir fate.
There the Prophet's words came to my ears.
There the Blessed One became...

... into the hearts of the people.

E knew that eir words would not be enough. Though many bluster, few take action and enact the changes that are needed to move the world forward. E came to know...

E came to know that eir words would need to lead to action. Thus E entrusted them to me.

E spoke these words to me:

"Faith without action is no faith. The words spoken must represent their true meaning and intent or they are no more than empty sounds. If one speaks and then acts in congruence, that is reverence. If one acts for the good of the whole, that is virtue. If one seeks perfection without causing attention, that is righteousness."

I felt upon me the heavy burden of wisdom and agreed...

...was my sacred covenant with em.

Then was I instructed these things:
To remember the name of the Prophet.
To write down the history of eir awakening.
To learn the meaning of eir words.
To apply that meaning to my life.
To teach others to do the same.
To spread that teaching wherever I would go.

# Chapter Fifteen

## She Spins, She Spins

Pa'kevutu: The Island Of Keshon

It was pandemonium when we arrived. There was confusion and fear in the faces of those who ran by us. Kim and I stopped to look around and catch our breath. It wasn't a hard place to find. All we had to do was follow the smoke... and the screaming. In front of us loomed a factory, three buildings made mostly of brick angled upward with four enormous smokestacks, a few windows, and the logo of some Corp I did not recognize. Behind them was a fourth building of painted brick with several windows on top, probably an administration site.

"Over there, look," Kim pointed.

In the distance stood a man gaving instructions to others. It looked like he had on a uniform kevan. I figured he was probably from the local security division now under the control of the Savuran corp.

"Let's go," I said to Kim.

We arrived and stood before him waiting our turn to speak to him.

"We need firans putting down streams in those corners there and there," the man said, pointing.

He was young with a face that was stretched with concern and uncertainty.

"I don't care!" the man barked at another stranger who appeared from the crowd. "I don't want anyone going in there until we know the building is safe to enter, understand?" He turned to another face nearby. "I need a list of all the employees and anyone else who may have been in those buildings and a list of those who have been accounted for, got it?" The other person acknowledged the order and disappeared. The man turned to see if anyone else needed his attention, No one spoke. This was our chance, I thought. I decided to be official.

"Excuse us, officer," I said, approaching him. "May we ask you some questions?"

"Who are you?"

"I am Detective Exizoyn One from Savuran and this is my partner Detective Uekimoy Three."

Kim tried hard not to flinch.

"Savuran? I don't recognize you," the officer said.

"We're from Yakrutich."

"Ah, big city detectives. What are you doing here?"

"We came to help you find the person responsible for this act."

"You have reason to believe this was not an accident?"

"We do," I said.

"Care to share?"

"We are not at liberty to speak of the details at this time," I said, trying not to sound too pompous.

"I see," said the officer. "You have a suspect?"

"We do."

"Let me guess, you're not at liberty to share that either?"

"Not at this time."

"I see," the man said. He gave us a sour look. "Then how can I help the big city detectives?"

"Did you know anything about this factory?"

"Just that they made some kind of solar device."

"Can you tell us anything else about it?"

"Not at this time," he smirked.

I shot a false grin back to him to let him know I was aware of his jab. "Were you aware that this factory may have been leaking lead contaminants, possibly into the air or into other substances?"

His smile dropped. "No, I wasn't."

Kim and I looked at each other then I turned my attention back to the officer.

"Was there any..." I began.

"No, no! Not over there, over there!" he shouted over our heads and pointed with his fingers. He turned his attention back to us.

"Was there any warning before the explosion?" I completed my question.

"I'm told there was a fire alarm that went off just before it happened. We've had only a few reports of casualties. I think most everyone was evacuated safely."

"Well, thank goodness for that," Kim muttered.

"Anything else I can do for you detectives? I'm kind of busy here." the officer said.

"Just keep your eyes and ears open," I said.

"That's my job, ma'am," he said with some pride.

I looked around. "And from the looks of it you seem to doing a good one."

"Thank you and good luck," he said then ran off toward some workers.

I turned and walked away with Kim close at my side.

"Detective Uekimoy?" she asked.

"Well, you were once a detective."

"Of sorts, and in a Corp that no one was supposed to know existed."

"Good times, eh?" I laughed.

"Yeah, good times," she mocked. "You got a plan?"

"We've got to get inside of one of those buildings. We should probably start with the central one.

"But you heard the man. They're not letting anyone in."

"We'll just have to find a way."

Kim walked a few paces. "You think he's still in there?" she asked.

"Maybe. Or maybe we'll find some evidence as to where he went or what he plans to do."

We went back to the complex and searched the area. The central building seemed less conspicuous than its two neighbors but its location would have been the best location for a bomb to have maximum effect. Kim found one of only a few ground-level windows and flagged me over. We paced back and forth near the window trying to look like we were doing something useful until we could find a moment when no one was near. We pushed aside glass shards protruding from the edges of the shattered window until we could safely go through it.

The inside of the building looked like everyone had decided to go on lunch break together. Chairs and desks filled the floor and each was topped with personal belongings and work items. Windows were broken, there was dust in the air, and items had fallen to the floor but, otherwise, the room was not damaged.

"I thought he might go for maximum effect," I said.

"Hit the central building and take it all down." Kim said. "Doesn't look here like the results of that plan."

"He must have gone for the production building then."

"The one with the chimneys?"

"Yeah. This way."

We headed for the larger building. Within minutes of running down soot-filled corridors we reached an outside door. I opened it to get a look outside then I shut it.

"Thought I heard voices," Kim whispered.

"Yeah. Couldn't see anyone but sounds like they're near. Can't run across the courtyard but I thought I saw a connector up a couple of flights."

Kim nodded and we turned back. We searched through several doorways until we found a set of stairs and made our way up. On the second floor the corridor stretched out over the courtyard toward the other building and sunlight streamed into its windows. Kim looked ready to run through it but I held her back. The other end was dark so it was hard to estimate the possible damage.

"Stay to the sides," I told her. "They should be stronger."

We moved along the sides of the corridor. Kim stayed closed behind me. Suddenly, the floor gave way beneath her and I had to catch her before her feet slipped through. I pulled her back up into the corridor.

"Thanks," she said peering down the hole. Brick fragments fell to the ground below. We continued, though more slowly, until we reached the end of the corridor. There was barely enough light from the high open windows to allow us a view of the main room. The building was mostly an empty shell. Anything not bolted down was thrown to the sides from the force of the blast.

"We'll have to climb down," I said, noticing an abundance of pipes and other footholds in the wall. "Just be slow and careful."

I remember we both slipped as we grabbed on to loose bricks or bent pipes but, otherwise, the climb was not too treacherous for either one of us. At the bottom we surveyed the damage together in silence. There were pipes, machinery parts, workplace items, and a variety of other unidentifiable equipment strewn across the floor.

"Looks like he…" Kim started to say but I stopped with a finger held across my lips.

I thought I heard something from inside the building.

It was muffled and soft like a kind of whimpering. I strained my ears to listen. I heard it again. Kim gave me a look to confirm she heard it too. I flashed her some hand signs to indicate where I thought it was coming from and how we should approach it. I would come from one side while she would come from the other. We stepped lightly until we came to a doorway and stopped.

There was a repeated whispering of words. I closed my eyes and shut out every other sound so I could hear them.

"Sheep sins, sheep sins…" The words continued. "She shayda threads."

That couldn't be right, I thought. Kim started to say something but I shook my head and listened again. The phrase came again.

"She spins, she spins…. (something, something,) weaves and threads…"

I couldn't make it out. I let out a frustrated but quiet sigh then I crouched down close to the ground. It sounded to me like the person was speaking downward, maybe at the floor. I put my ear down low and hoped that some of the flooring might reflect the words back to me. I adjusted my angle and waited for the next iteration.

"She spins, she spins, she warps and weaves." I smiled and listened for the rest. "She shapes the threads of florid dreams."

I smiled again because I recognized the words but then my smile faded when the speaking stopped and sobbing took its place.

I peeked in and saw someone crouched over a body on the ground. The person over the body was making soft noises. His shoulders jumped with each quiet outburst. He was crying. I stepped sideways until I was fully in the doorframe and whoever was beyond it would see me. Kim put a hand on my shoulder to stop me and pull me back but I remained. As I moved, some rubble moved under my feet. The crying man heard it and stopped. He turned himself around just enough to see me.

It was him. It was Awri.

# Chapter Sixteen

## *The Lumen of Truth*

From The Chronicles Of Enlightenment

*Editor's Note: This manuscript describes the death of the Prophet and how it influenced the Revealer to begin his mission. It was discovered on the Island of Keshon. It is written in a manner that became progressively more obscure as the author's writing continued.*

In the great hall, The Prophet received.
The Angels of Paradise raised voices in joy.
The revelations fulfilled.
The Prophet received the words of The Enlightened One
And in his heart growen and flourish.
The dawning of renewal would be upon the land.

I knew the blessed prophet a short time
Yet more full and rich than any other.
At death revealed the truth of the universe,
Told to me.
At death not of one person but of an era,
An artificial but meaningful mark of time-
Mere signpost.

The Prophet died, I died inside.
The world went from colorful to dark
From ignorance to fear.
Nothing but final words sounded;
A face of calm assent.
He accepted the fate.

I did not.
I cried against:
The injustice of the moment,
The order of the universe,

The meaning of death.

I thought I understood these things.
I did not.
When eir words spoken,
Only then came the understanding.

Ceorans tell us:
Life has meaning
When we pursue Perfection
In the model of the Corp.
Death interrupts us.
Death is why we never reach full perfection.

We strive to be:
The perfect Citran,
The perfect model of the company sosh,
The perfect tenants of elusive fields of paradise.

When a Citran dies,
We are saddened by the disruption.
Hundreds have died to become the perfection.
Hundreds have a child or two
To carry on that pursuit.
Hundreds told lives have meaning.
Hundreds told deaths have meaning
But never told the meaning itself.

What gives life meaning?
Not happiness.
Ite self aggrandizing, selfish,
Invitation to the intoxicating powers of gluttony and sloth,
The end to the dedicated worker.
Life ite meaning,
Life striven for Perfection
Life in pursuit of Paradise,
The source of all love,
Beauty, Joy, Peace,
Meaning,
Happiness,
The beginning and the end,

E said that life defines death.
These words thundered me.
The Prophet reached the ground beneath me,

Pulled ite out.
I was sent to darkness.
I did not understand.

They said death defines life.
We are judged by the dictates of the Corp.
Those who succeed are models for us all.
We are nearly perfect, they claim.
We look forward to that moment,
But if life defines death,

There ite meaning to life.
But I could not see this
Until the clouds cleared my eyes.
I could not do this
Until the clouds cleared my heart.
The lumen of truth had yet
To be.

# Chapter Seventeen

## The Weave of the Cloth

Pa'kevutu: The Island Of Keshon

The room was dark and drifting clouds of dust made it difficult to see inside but a single shaft of light poured down from above. It caught the brilliance of the late day sun and formed it into a line of white that cut across the room at a steep angle. A swath of it ran across the face of my old friend, the contours of which melded the harsh lines of the beam to the curves of his forehead and chin. In that frame was sadness and agony streaked with soft tears.

"I didn't mean to hurt anyone," he sobbed.

I stepped into the room and headed toward him. "I know, Awri."

"They were killing people and I just wanted to make them stop."

"I know, Awri," I repeated, softer. I took another slow step toward him. "Is he...?" I said, nodding toward the floor.

Awri lowered his head. I took another step. I heard Kim slip in behind me.

"Awri," I said. "We need to get you out of here."

Awri raised his head again. "They were killing their own people. For the sake of the Corp."

I took another step. "Awri, listen to me. Very soon this place is going to be flooded with officials from every security and safety corp on the island. You need to come with us and we'll get this all sorted out."

"They can't see what's happening here." he said. "They place their lives, their trust, their future into the hands of the Corp. The Corp wraps those hands in a cloth of belief, a theology they claim imbibes a grand metaphysical significance to them. The cloth is soft, warm, comforting yet it slowly crushes your spirit and self-worth until you are nothing more than another thread mixed into the weave."

"Awri, please, come with us."

"The weave of the cloth of the Dreamweaver," Awri whispered.

"What?" Kim said.

"I have to tell them," Awri went on. "They need to know what is happening to them. It is what I was destined to do. The message of Ishlan is meant to free the people."

I took another step. "And if people die along the way, it's OK, right? As long as the mission is being fulfilled, the message delivered. How does that make you any different from them?"

His eyes narrowed. "Because I care. That's the difference, the only important difference. I care. I care that someone got hurt. I care that people are being used. Whether it's for the purpose of the Prophet or for the Corps, it doesn't matter. I care."

"OK, then," I said. "Don't let it end here. Let us help you get this cleared up and you can go on your way. You can continue on your journey."

"My journey," Awri repeated then turned his attention back to the body slumped on the floor. "My journey ends here."

With his back turned I took a slow but long step in his direction.

"It doesn't have to," I said. "You can continue on to wherever..."

"A new journey. It is just beginning," he whispered. He lowered his hands to the inert face peering up at him and cupped its cheeks. "I know now what I must do, where I must go."

I took another long step but he turned his head back to me.

"I saw him," Awri said.

"Who, Awri? Who did you see?" I said.

"Ishlan, the Prophet of Kugoya," Awri whispered with reverence. He turned his attention back to the face in his hands. "E came to me... in this face. I saw eir passing all over again. Now I understand... I understand what E was trying to say... Perfection! Perfection is the whole and when we reach it... we become part of the whole. The stream meets the ocean. The whisper becomes the wind... We become em... E becomes us... I saw em because E is all of us."

Kim came close behind me. "What in the name of the Seven Sisters is he babbling on about?" she said. I put a hand up to silence her.

"E showed me my destiny," Awri said, still looking down.

I took another small step. I was getting close. "What is it, Awri? What's your destiny?"

"The spinner of things, the weaver of dreams, the spiral of Perfection."

Kim rolled her eyes. "We're not going to get anywhere with him. He's delusional."

I ignored her. I knew there was something to what he said.

"Awri!" I said. He was staring at the dead face. "Awri, did you see the Dreamweaver?"

He turned his head slowly toward me. "Kwanchu," he said. "Kwanchu is where I will fulfill my purpose."

"Kwanchu?" I asked. "The island of Kwanchu is your destiny?"

I moved to take another step, one I was sure would get me close enough to grab him or knock him down but he turned back so fast it caught me off guard. By the time I realized what had happened there was a handbow with its dart pointed at my throat and at the end of that handbow was Awri.

"Yes, Kwanchu," he said. "That is where I must go. That is where I must spread the message of the Prophet and I cannot let anyone stop me."

"But why there?" I asked. "What's so special about Kwanchu?"

"I don't know. Not all things have been revealed. He tells me what I need to know when I need to know it."

"And right now he's telling you, through some dead person, to go to the northernmost island so you can crawl around on steep mountain peaks full of ice and snow to look for some dreaming person. Doesn't sound like a wise idea for a prophet," mocked Kim.

Awri moved the handbow from in front of me and toward Kim. "It is not for you to understand. You are not a Seeker."

"Look, pal," said Kim. "I may not be some Seeker of Perfection or even of mediocrity but I do seek the truth and I know the truth doesn't come from the mouths of dead people. Maybe you should..."

She was distracting him, giving me a chance to move in since I was closer. I took the hint and waited for the right opportunity to act. His body faced Kim which left me an opening. All I needed to do was slide in just a little bit further... A second handbow rose to meet me and I stopped. I had to smile, though. I was the one who had trained him so many yerons ago.

Awri turned his head slowly to my direction.

"I'm sorry," he said. I wasn't sure if he was apologizing for what he had done or what he was about to do.

"I thought you didn't want to hurt anyone," I said to him.

"I don't," he said.

"Then why are you pointing weapons at us?"

"You know why. I can't let you take me away right now. What I have to do is more important than my own life. The world must know what I can teach them. I can help end the futility, the hopelessness. The world needs... hungers for the words of the Prophet."

"What about our lives, Awri? What good is a message of the hopefulness of life if everyone has to die to hear it?"

"All change requires sacrifice," he said.

"Awri, listen to me," I pleaded with him. "If you start killing people you will be on every Fugitive Sought list on every island and the mainland. You won't be able to hide anywhere. You'll be chased down from the Eastern Wall to the Western Wall, from the sewers of Sychkin to the swamps of Lysalo. You'll have nowhere to hide. How are you going to convince the people that you're right. Why would they listen to some apostle accused of criminal actions? Why would anyone have any reason to believe you?"

Awri didn't move. His eyes remained focused on mine but I could tell there was an internal war going on behind them. I tried to help him take sides.

"Awri... Shorix... You were once my partner. You were a great detective. You saved lives and helped people." I paused. "This isn't you... this isn't who you are... Let us help you." I reached my hand out. "We'll work to clear your name of this mess. We'll prove that this Corp let its workers and the community die and that you were just trying to stop the killing... Just... Just come with us."

*My sweet granddaughter, I remember what happened next so clearly because it defined to me what this man had become.*

I remember his eyes never left mine. Instead, he looked right into me or, maybe, he looked through me into the next moment, I'm not sure. All I know is that he never took his gaze from me as he let the arm with the handbow pointed at my chest arc down toward the ground. He kept the other weapon pointed at Kim, though. When the hand nearest to me was almost to the ground I stepped in to grab him but, again, I was taken by surprise.

His intention was clear from the start though I never saw it until I was unable to prevent it from happening. He never was going to let me take him. His motion was designed to get me to step a little closer, just as I did. He wanted me at point-blank range. He didn't want to miss and he didn't.

He raised the handbow back up faster than I could have imagined and released its small quiver. The dart entered my left shoulder with such force that I was spun around and thrown to the ground. Next he released the dart pointed at Kim but she was already in motion. He missed her but sent her scrambling away which is probably what he intended. He was clear enough of both of us that he was able to run toward an open doorway and escape.

"No! Not again," I yelled and tried to go after him but the pain in my shoulder told me otherwise. Any other quick motions now would only bring on further damage. I dropped to one knee in agony. Kim was further away but was determined to try and go after him. The problem was that he slammed shut the door to the corridor and blocked it off with some heavy object. By the time she caught up to him he was through it.

"Damn it!" she yelled as she pounded her fist into the door. "Isn't there some other way I could go? Maybe I could catch up to him in another hallway."

"We don't know which way he's going."

"There has to be something I can do to catch up to him."

"He'll be long gone before you can find a way around." I said with a groan. "You think you can help me up?"

She turned to me and looked at the dart in my shoulder. "Yeah, yeah, yeah, sorry. Sometimes I get a little too focused on the chase." She walked toward me.

"You don't have to remind me," I said.

Kim took my good arm and lifted me up. The pain was excruciating but I was determined not to let it stop me.

"C'mon," said Kim. "Let's get that taken care of. We'll plug that hole and put a little ice on that shoulder and you'll be fine."

"That's good. I hear there's a lot of ice where we're going."

Kim moved me toward a fallen beam and helped me sit down. I tried to keep from passing out. The room began to swirl and I took in some deep breaths to steady myself. The ground became a blur of shapes and images. At that moment something caught my eye. There was a pile of crumpled papers not far from the body on the floor where I had seen Awri. The pile caught my attention because the papers looked out of place. They were not dusty or burnt. They were clean and crisp.

I took another deep breath and cleared my head. "What's that?" I said, pointing to the papers.

Kim followed my finger until she could see where I was pointing. I could tell she was thinking the same as me. She walked to them, picked them up and began reading. She stopped and looked at me.

"Gibberish." she said.

"What is it?" I asked.

"Some meaningless rambling about the universe and..." She read on but then put the papers down. "I have no idea."

"May I?" I said, holding out my hand.

Kim handed them to me and I read one of them.

"It's his handwriting," I said.

"That crazy guy we were just chasing?"

"Yeah. He wants us to follow him."

"What?" Kim laughed. "Then why shoot us and run away?"

I looked at the papers again. "I don't know. We'll find out when we visit the land of dreams."

# Chapter Eighteen

## *The Cyclonus*

### From The Chronicles Of Enlightenment

*Editor's Note: This manuscript is sometimes subtitled The Cyclonus: Profound Simplicity. It is a collection of teachings in poetic form. Awrithrich the Revealer claimed that these were the words of the Prophet as spoken to him before his death but the history is murky. Little has been recorded of Ishlan's actual words and the Revealer spent little time with him. It is more likely that many of these words were given to the Revealer at a much later date. Whether they were spoken by Ishlan emself or were eir own insights attributed to Ishlan is a matter of speculation. The Revealer has claimed that the Prophet spoke to him in a distorted language because E was so close to the sacred truth that the words were difficult to convey. Regardless, the texts certainly come from a time closer to the final days of the Revealer because of the particular language used. The texts that have come down to us are entered here in their original form. Likely translations of each are given below.*

From the seed of possibility grows potentiality.  The blessed prophet came to know great truth and spread it throughout the world.
Eir words echoed through the valleys and across the peaks of mountains.
It calmed the churning waters and hushed the violent tempest.
When E was done speaking,
E died so that E could become the truth
And not just the words.
E travelled to Paradise and knew Perfection
So that all others who followed em would know it.
The masses who surrounded em and mourned eir death
Rejoiced in eir revelation.

I am the Revealer.

I am the one to bring truth to you.
Hear what the Prophet has taught me:

1.
Seek not in look
Nor looked.
Meaning in life.
Not ite bought
Nor crystal shinen.
Life ese meaning.
Corps ite not.
Nor playen.
Life ese meaning.
Not ite eaten foods.
Nor drunken elixir.
Life ese meaning.
Not ite obsession
Nor obsession source.
Life ese meaning.
Not ite told tale
Nor others you story.
Life ese meaning.
Not ite own held
Nor ite sent.
Life ese meaning.
Not ite dawn glory
Nor dusk calm
Nor the cyclonus between.
Ite ese grasping simple
Life ese meaning.


2.
Once sought the true tree
In true shade
In true covering
At trunk
And true branches holden
And true leaves on branches
Waven
And coolen,
And true fruit feeden
And true water grass
On its roots.
Thirst quenched.

Once sought the true tree
Soothen my abrasions.
Once sought the true tree
With many on every land.
North trees
Tall and thin
And soft place sitten.
Yukree trees mighty
Long branches, wide leaves
And shade given.
Western Island trees
Strong and fruitful
And nectar succulence filled.
Warm shore trees
Wonder twisted shapes
And pointed ways.
But none were true,
One more than one,
One all of all.

The true tree ite not one,
Ite ese all.
Each tree a leaf of the true tree
And the true tree a branch of the great truth.

3.
Multitude of no one.
But no one can walk the path.
No child ite parent.
One tree roots hold
No path walker blazes.
Sea risen fallen ot.
First weak then strong then weak.
We risen fallen ot.

4.
Once seen a flower beautiful.
Oh to gaze it ever.
Sunshine-fire colors
Delighted mists fragrance.
Petals delicate, soft.
But danger touch of destruction.
Ite opened
And petals wide spreaden

Holding three jewels.
Prima fell apart:
Impermanence.
Seconda in two parts,
One more than one
But spun even:
Balance.
Tertia large,
Its own flower large,
With faces in all ways.
All the flower seen within
Until all flower brilliant light
In all directions,
All things reflected:
Interconnection.

These were the words delivered to me.
I pass them to all who will listen.
Many will be unable to hear them.
The truth can be harsh and difficult.
It upends a life lived long in ignorance.
It delivers a destination without a smooth route.
It paints gray pictures in new colors.
I spoke to the people and delivered the truth.

When at first the world learned of the truth, they could not accept it.
They wanted it to go away.
They wanted to return to the ignorance they once knew
But the truth of eternal light cannot be vanquished.
It must be revealed.

Now you seek the truth.
You have come to this work seeking answers
Because you feel an emptiness inside
And you want to fill it.

You seek the garden,
though you walk a cobbled path,
but the feast is already set before you.
All you need do is taste!

*Editor's Note: The following are translations of the four revealed texts above.*

1.
The purpose you seek is not found where you look.
It is not in your looks nor your stature.
Life itself has meaning.
It is not bought with credits
Nor found in bright crystals.
Life itself has meaning.
It is not found in the Corp
Nor even on the playground.
Life itself has meaning.
It is not in the meals you prepare
Nor the intoxicating drink.
Life itself has meaning.
It is not in the thing obsessed
Nor in the reason for the obsessing.
Life itself has meaning.
It is not in the story you tell
Nor of the story told of you.
Life itself has meaning.
It cannot be held in possession
Nor can it be given away.
Life itself has meaning.
It is not in the glory of dawn
Nor in the calm dusk
Nor the myriad of risings and fallings between.
It is the simple understanding that
Life itself has meaning.


2.
Once I sought the perfect tree
With perfect shade
And perfect covering to hold me
At its trunk

And perfect branches to embrace me
And perfect leaves along those branches
To wave at me
And keep me cool,
With perfect fruit to feed me
And dew on the grasses
That grows on its roots
To quench my endless thirst.

I sought the perfect tree

To soothe my imperfections.

I searched on every land and found many.
The trees of the north
Were tall and thin
And offered a soft place to sit.
The mighty trees of the Yukree
Grew long branches and wide leaves
And gave me shade from the sun.
The strong trees of the Western Islands
Filled with moist fruit
Sated me with succulence
And sweet nectar.
The trees of warm shores
In their twisted shapes of wonder
Pointed the way to follow.
But none were the perfect tree,
One greater than the others,
The culmination of all.

The perfect tree cannot be found in a single example.
It is found in them all.
Each tree is but a leaf of the great tree
And the great tree is but a branch of perfection.

3.
We are alone amidst the multitude.
The path is yours but it cannot be taken alone.
A child cannot raise itself.

Many roots hold a single tree.
One cannot, at the same time, blaze a trail and walk it.
The sea moves by rising and falling.
We begin in weakness, grow in strength, then end in weakness.
Like the sea, we move by rising and falling.

4.
Once, I came upon a flower so beautiful,
I could not stop looking at it.
Its colors blazed in the sunshine.
Its fragrance filled me with delight.
Its petals were so delicate and soft.
I wanted to touch them but was afraid
Of destroying it.
Then, as I stared on it,

The flower opened
And spread its petals wide.
In its soft center the flower held three jewels.
I reached for them.
The first fell apart at my touch.
It was the jewel of impermanence.
The second jewel was in two parts:
One larger than the other.
Though it appeared uneven
It was as one entity when spun.
It was the jewel of balance.
The third jewel was nearly as large as the flower itself
And was multi-faceted.
It reflected all parts of the flower within itself
Until the image came together as one brilliant light.
No matter where I looked at this stone,
I could see the reflection of all things.
This was the jewel of interconnectivity.

# Chapter Nineteen

## Hide and Seek

Pa'kevutu: The Island Of Kwanchu    The Academy Of Research In
Delia

I thought he might be dead. His face was almost perfectly round. His head was topped with two splashes of thinning gray hair connected by a few thin filaments across the top. I found myself staring at those hairs. I wanted to ask him why he didn't just cut them off but I was afraid he would be insulted. There was no need to insult him but the urge to point out those rogue hairs out was powerful, overwhelming. I'm sure he wouldn't answer anyway. It was possible those gray strands were the only thing holding together the other two islands of hair floating on his balding head.

It was easy to focus on that barren landscape because the rest of his face didn't move. Lines formed on it from years of pouring over great tomes of collected wisdom but those lines did not move. His full round eyes were surrounded by puffy bags of splotched skin and they, too, did not move, not even to blink. Maybe he was dead. Maybe we walked in on him in his last moments of life. He could have had a stroke or a heart attack just before we entered the room, maybe as we climbed the old stone stairs. His last moments may have been filled by the sound of two strangers coming to stare at his hair.

I knew so little about the legend of the Dreamweaver and her home island of Kwanchu. I knew we had to learn more so we found a ship that would take us to the island. We arrived in the southern port town of Nomenk with the vision of snow-capped mountains behind it. Soon the whole island would be covered in snow and ice but, for now, the port was still open and the roads clear. From the town of Nomenk, filled with its tourist attractions and traveler's accommodations, we traveled North to the village of Delia.

Few visitors to the island went this way. Most stayed in the southern half of Kwanchu and followed along the main road to the town of Padhu or ventured to the beautiful seaside village of Azenda but any treks to the North included the risk of being trapped in snow-bound old taverns or, worse, caught in the open without any shelter at all. Kwanchu was a tough place, a good place to hide, a good place to foster different ways of thinking.

*I know, my dear granddaughter, that you have never been to Kwanchu though I am sure that one day you will go there. Let me take this chance to describe it to you.*

It is the northernmost island in Pa'Kavutu. I've already told you about how it can get quite cold and snow-bound but I haven't described the immense beauty of the island. On its outer edges are ports and beaches and the well-known high plains plateau with its sharp cliffs that can be seen for miles from the sea. The rest of the island is mostly thick forest and tall mountains. Three different mountain ranges run across its surface roughly from West to East. It has only one main road with a central ring that connects the island's main towns and villages. It is a breathtaking though dangerous place to visit and I hope you will find yourself able to see it someday. But I digress.

On with the story...

We found ourselves in the small village of Delia because I remembered that it was the home of one of the few Academies of Research in Pa'Kevutu and was the only one in Kwanchu. We made our way to the Academy and asked for directions to the Philosophy Division. After more searching, hunting, and questioning, we found ourselves inside this old stone building and this tiny cramped room. It was the office and study of the Most High Scholan, Master Porfyndal Three.

As you might expect, the room was filled with books on nearly every wall. The dark wood used for the bookshelves–which were the walls themselves–made the room feel dim and mysterious. The only light in the room came from two small windows on either side of the inert professor. The window to the right faced North and provided a view of Lake Brelna, the largest on the island, and several peaks of the central mountain ranges. The window to the left looked down on the dusty streets and ramshackle buildings of Delia. In between those diametric views sat the professor in his chair, motionless. I thought again he might just be dead in his chair as his life's story passed before his cloudy eyes.

Enough, I thought. We have been sitting here biding our time looking at every part of this room and the views through the windows while we wait for this person to speak. We have waited long enough. No more protocol!

"Master Porfyndal," I said. "I am Detective Exi and this is my partner Detective Kim. We have come to ask you some questions about an ongoing investigation we are pursuing."

"Hmm?" the old man hummed. The two large orbs that were his eyes moved in across the space of the room until they fell on me. There they remained, unmoving.

I looked at Kim. She looked back at me and tilted her head. I decided to press on.

"Professor, it's about the Dreamweaver cult. We were told that you were the one…"

Suddenly the stolid face twitched and tilted. His eyebrows furled and narrowed but no words passed his lips.

I waited a moment for him to speak but nothing happened. I could see Kim getting impatient.

"Can you help us Professor?" Kim said.

At any other time she might have thrown in a few expletives and carefully crafted nicknames but she was holding back. She knew, as did I, that this strange man might be our only chance of finding Awri.

"Hmm?" came the sound again as the head adjusted position to take notice of Kim.

"Can… you… help… us?" Kim intoned. She was getting to the end of her rope. She might have leapt across the great wooden desk and sent dozens of books sliding across it and onto the floor had not a tiny smile come across the professor's lips. It caught her off guard.

He turned back to me. "You came here to ask about fairy tales?"

The company line. Now it was my turn to smile.

"She spins she spins, she warps and weaves. She shapes the threads of florid dreams," I recited.

The professor's smile slackened.

"I don't remember the rest," I said. "But I know that the myth of the Dreamweaver is more than just a simple fairy tale."

"How do you know this?" the old man whispered. "Very few know the ancient rhymes."

"Call it a hobby of mine," I said.

"Some people collect buttons. She collects scraps of arcane theology," Kim quipped.

The Master said nothing but now there was a strain of fear added to the stoic face.

"Look, Professor," I said. "I know you probably have an arrangement with the Academy that allows you to research the cult so long as you do not divulge any of your findings to the public. The Corps do not want any competing ideologies. I understand. You're afraid your agreement will be in jeopardy or you might even think we are Corp spies here to test you."

"I cannot share any information with you," he said.

"We think someone's life may be at stake here," I said.

The man did nothing for several moments, then spoke, "Are you two really detectives?"

I reached into the front pouch of my kevan and pulled out my Savuran Identification Badge. Even though I was off the force it was never taken from me and, somehow, I couldn't leave it behind. The professor took the badge and looked it over.

"You're a long way from home, Detective," he said, handing it back to me.

"Yes, I am," I said.

"This investigation must be very important to you, then," he said.

Of course he figured out what was going on. He was a highly ranked academy researcher. Like me, he was trained to piece together disparate clues and figure out how they were supposed to come together. He knew I was out of my jurisdiction. He knew I was not in his office for any official business but he also knew the badge was real.

"Yes," I said. "Vitally important."

He looked at me then smiled but it was a smile that lit up more than his face. His whole body became animated. His body forgot about those years and regained a youthful exuberance.

"I may not be able to tell you anything but you are official workers of the Council. I cannot keep you from searching the premises."

His eyes remained fixed on mine as if they were waiting for a signal that I might understand but I was unsure. I looked at Kim to see if she had any inkling of his intentions. She didn't. As if he had suddenly came upon a new theory, he jumped up from his desk and bounded toward his shelves full of weighty books.

Granddaughter, it was a sight to watch this small elderly man fly from shelf to shelf as he grabbed great tomes of wisdom and toss them on his desk. It was like watching a great conductor bring together different instruments in a beautiful symphony of words and pictures. Each book was a small part of the symphonic masterpiece. I don't know how long we watched him grab books, tear open their covers, and flip pages. His fingers danced on those papers as a pianist might caress the keys of the instrument.

"This one," he would say as he reached for another book. "And this one," or "Mustn't forget this one," he would mumble at another.

Finally, he stopped and admired his work. He was done. There on his desk was his masterpiece and he stared at it with pride. He said nothing and stepped away to a corner of his office where he placed a stool and sat. It was our turn now.

Kim and I took his former position behind the desk and peered over the books. They were strewn across the desk in great heaps. All were open to specific pages so that bits of each peered out from behind dark and dusty covers. Two books were open and on top of the rest. We started there.

Kim read out loud: "The Cult of the Dreamweaver. Small bands of people on a few islands who believe they are the keepers of an ancient wisdom. They insist their religion was the original theology of Perfection adopted and altered during the rise of the Corp system." She put her finger on the page and let it slide down as she scanned the words. "Doesn't say what they believe," she commented.

I turned the book in front of me so that I could read it. My eyes found a familiar passage. "Listen to this," I said. "She spins she spins, she warps and weaves. She shapes the threads of florid dreams."

"I've heard that before," Kim said.

"It goes on," I responded, then read on. "From true ideal to mere reflection, she crafts the world into Perfection."

Kim pushed a few books aside and searched for more clues. "Got something here," she said. "Says here: 'the worshippers of the Dreamweaver believe that all manifestations of reality are mere images of their counterparts in...' I don't understand this part."

"Skip it and go on."

Kim read some more to herself then spoke. "Something about how all the things we see are imperfect copies of perfect ideals envisioned and made real by the Dreamweaver."

"The Creatrix," I whispered.

"What?" said Kim.

"Nothing. Here look at this," I said, pushing aside another book to reveal an image I noticed. Before me was the symbol I had encountered only a few times before. "The Eltry," I said. "The symbol of the cult."

Kim looked over my shoulder. "It's described as: 'Three spiral arms that join together and with different symbols at their far ends.' But what does it mean?"

I read further down the page. "Here it is. Something about each arm represents one of three elements: fire, water, and stone and the Dreamweaver lives at the confluence of these three."

"A location?" Kim asked.

I shot a glance toward the professor. He was grinning as if two of his favorite pupils had just graded well on an exam.

"Keep looking," I said.

We shuffled through books and glanced at passages until Kim said, "This might be it." She pointed to a page in another book and read it. "The temple of the cult is at the meeting of three rivers."

"I didn't know they had a temple. Is there a map in this pile?"

"Maybe," Kim said shuffling some books around. "Look... here." She pointed to a section of a map of Kwanchu.

"Well, I'll be... I never noticed that before."

Kim's finger rested at a point where two rivers in the Vipya Province joined together to make a third. The place where the rivers came together was surrounded by three mountains.

"That's where he'll be," I said.

"How do you know?" Kim asked.

"Because he will be asking the same questions we just did." I closed the book and looked hard at the old man in the corner of the room. My glance drained whatever spirit he had left, whatever energy he had used in the sojourn through his books. He was back to looking barely alive. He lowered his head to nap and those two hairs glared back at me.

"How do you know that?" Kim asked.

"Because I trained him," I said, not taking my eyes from the professor. "And because he was here too." From underneath several of the books I pulled out a few sheets of paper and handed them to Kim.

"Let me guess," Kim said. "He left us a love letter."

# Chapter Twenty

## *The River of Souls*

**From The Chronicles Of Enlightenment**

*Editors Note: The following manuscript is believed to be the final revelation given to the Revealer. A likely translation is below.*

The day came.
The Prophet delivered his understanding,
He extended his arms.
He called to the angels to take him back to Paradise.
He gave to me his final words.

(Original:)
River soules whol,
A bankes sandishol.
Flowen ot,
Risen ot,
So divi.
Ite lodriftes,
Ite seekes ite.
La divi ta burneshart.
River in prima,
Morfa in en.

(Translation:)
The river of souls is whole
Though its sandy banks are shallow.
It flows out, rises above itself, becomes many.
Through its many meanderings,
The multitude seeks the source.
Those who yearn to find the river
In the beginning,
Become it in the end.

# Chapter Twenty-One

## Fire, Water, and Stone

Pa'kevutu: The Island Of Kwanchu   Vipyu Province

From Delia we traveled the main road west as it snaked its way around Lake Brelna. We entered the Delbrin Mountain range. When the road began to turn north, we followed a river heading West into the snow-capped mountains. It took us the better part of a day to get through the high-walled canyons until we reached a point where the river disappeared into the rocks. There we camped for the night with some supplies we bought in Delia. Kim and I huddled around a warm fire in a rock alcove on a cold night.

"You got a plan?" Kim asked, wrapped in a thin blanket.

"Just to get there," I said.

"And then what? You going to arrest Awri for setting off a bomb or are you going to recommend he be given a professorship at the Academy of Research in the Crazy-Talk Division."

"I don't know, Kim. I'm taking this one as it comes."

Kim wrapped her blanket around her tighter and shifted her weight. She stared into the fire. "Seems a little odd to me, that's all."

I didn't say anything to her. I grabbed a stick we broke from several fallen branches and threw it into the flames. Sparks jumped up and the fire danced as it illuminated Kim's face.

"What's the obsession, Exi?" Kim said.

"What do you mean?"

"In the name of the Seven Sisters! You're a Third Child! You could be like a superstar out there. You've interacted with the

Shadow-Keepers. People respect you, they listen to you. You could be a leader. Instead you're out here in the woods chasing this guy down... and for what?"

I grabbed another stick and swirled ashes aimlessly around the fire. The wood popped and snapped as it burned and the coals sizzled. "He was my partner, Kim."

"But he's not your partner anymore. He's chosen a new path," Kim said, then paused. "Exi, the Shadow-Keepers gave us a warning. They told us that if we didn't control our growth and development we would strangle ourselves. They weren't able to stop us and now they're not here anymore. Someone needs to give the people that message and the best person to do that is you."

I tore off tiny twigs from a branch and threw them into the fire. "I just need to know he's going to be alright, that's all... Are you coming with me or not?"

Kim let out a deep sigh before she propped herself against a rock wall and did her best to get comfortable. She was tired. We were both tired, but I couldn't sleep. She turned her head and closed her eyes. "Yeah," she said. "I'm coming with you."

I watched her fall to sleep as I kept the fire going then I gave in to my own exhaustion.

The next morning Kim and I followed the river into the mountain. It took us into a cavern. With fire-lit torches we walked in through dark corridors and watched the river slow and widen. It nearly turned into an underground lake except that a rising roar of sound told us otherwise. Light appeared at the far end of the cavern and the dry land ended. We had to swim to see what was on the other side.

"Waterfall?" Kim said looking toward the light.

"Would be my best guess. We'll have to swim but stay close to the edge. Grab whatever you can when you get to the opening."

"What if we get sucked into it and spit out like bad fruit?"

"My guess is that the water is so wide here because the cavern is acts like a dam. That means there should be a part of the wall that holds back some of the water. We need to get behind that."

"OK. I'll follow you." We checked our packs for loose items, wrapped them tight against the water, then tightened the straps. We stepped into the water and complained about the cold. We tried to walk along the edge until we couldn't any longer then moved into the water while we hugged the side walls.

The light was growing so we no longer needed our torches. The water widened even further as we were able to see through the opening and toward the sky. There was the form of another mountain beyond the opening but it was surrounded only by the blue of open air. There was no sight of any ground. The sound of water rushing over the rough rock and toward whatever was below grew louder until it became nearly deafening.

"Stay close!" I yelled, trying to control my chattering teeth.

Kim could barely hear me but understood what I meant. She nodded. We had to kick and splash hard to keep to the side of the water. It wanted to pull us into its center and toss us over the side.

Several times my hand slipped on the wet rock. Kim drifted out to help me move back to the side and then I had to pull her back toward me. She had her own troubles when her backpack got caught on a hidden branch and she couldn't reach around to free herself. I had to dive under the dark water to find the source of the snag. I yanked it free with barely a breath left in my lungs but I was able to do it. Kim pulled me up as I gasped for air.

Gradually the cavernous pond waters got calmer and we were able to drift to the far wall. By then the sound of falling water was nearly intolerable. We were already exhausted and took some time to catch our breath. We moved hand-over-hand to the opening and carefully peered below.

There was not one waterfall but many spread out along the wall of the mountain. Fortunately, though, we were not as high up as I feared. The land below us was rough which was a good thing for us. It meant we would have places to hold and step as we descended. Trees twisted along uneven rocky ledges in strange shapes and patterns would make it possible for us to hang on to different branches and crawl our way out of the cavern. We found a ledge nearby and stopped to view our surroundings.

I'm sure Kim was surprised to see the look on my face at that moment as she came up from behind me. It was an impressive sight beneath us, something I could never have imagined. We stared down into a valley formed at the base of three mountains. The water behind us fell out from several openings in the rock so that there were a myriad of fountains. The water trickled and thundered down the side of the many ledges and crags then collected itself into a river at the bottom. To our right stood another mountain but its face was made mostly of long stretches of bare rock. There was little space for trees to grow in those narrow ledges. It looked as if someone had cut into the round green mountain and exposed the hard stiff stone beneath. To our left was yet another mountain and it was shaped much like the one we were on only it had wide swaths of black forest on it. Perhaps it fell victim to lightning strikes since it was the highest of the three but it seemed as if it had received more than its fair share.

"Fire, water, and stone," Kim whispered.

"What?" I said.

She pointed to each mountain and muttered a single word. "Fire... water... and stone," she repeated.

I looked down to where the water collected and followed its path.

"The conjunction of three rivers," I said. It was my time to whisper. It somehow felt like we were on sacred ground.

The river below us came to meet another river from the South. Together the two combined to create yet a larger river that flowed West between the stone and the fire mountain, presumably toward the sea. Where the rivers joined together there was a small lake and in the midst of that lake was a tiny island covered in thick green plants and shrubs.

Kim and I looked at each other then moved to descend the mountain we were on. We knew where we needed to go.

At the bottom of the mountain we found the remains of an old footbridge across the river but it had been long ago washed away and destroyed. Now only but a few of the main supports were left standing in the dirt. There was no other way to cross the river to the island.

"And I just got my clothes dry," Kim said to the water.

We pulled our packs in tight then walked into the water. It wasn't much warmer than the mountain water and it felt as if we were being swallowed by ice. We swam across and walked onto the shore of the island. The scrubs and brush there were thick. Kim found a branch on the ground and used it to hack away at the weeds.

"Well, which way?" Kim asked.

"Toward the center, I would think," I said.

I looked for a branch as well and started to hack away at the greenery. We used the three mountains that glared down upon us from across each river to find our way to the center. The brush turned into trees that thickened the more we ventured inland. In time, our sticks became useless against the mangled branches and tall tree trunks. The canopy of leaves above us grew so thick it blocked out the sun and turned the area around us into a dark cavern of wood rather than stone. We worked our way as far inland as we could hoping that we were still moving in a straight line. Finally, the woods grew so thick and the forest so dark that we had to stop. Kim and I stood panting in what little room we had to stand.

"Well... what now?" Kim gasped.

"I don't... know," I said. "I'm all out of prophecy and scripture."

"I know what we need," Kim said as she moved to find a log to sit on. There was barely enough room to stand but she managed to find an outcropping of branches and sat on them. "What we need is one of those moments of dumb luck."

"Dumb luck?" I said. Shards of light streamed through small openings in the tree branches above us and created bands of brightness that danced on Kim's body.

"Yeah, you know," Kim said. "Haven't you ever read a story or heard a tale where somebody is looking for something and they can't find it and then something strange happens and they find it? That's dumb luck."

"Something strange?"

"Yeah, a rock falls from the sky or the wind just happens to blow the right way to reveal the answer to the riddle, that kind of thing."

I wanted to laugh, if for nothing else than I knew it would feel good to laugh at our own foolishness but something caught my eye. Kim moved her leg up a little to change her sitting position and in the process had unwittingly moved aside some vines. The bobbing and weaving patches of light illuminated the place her leg had exposed. There was something there that was not made of living growth.

"You mean like that?" I said, pointing to the spot under her leg.

Kim bent over to see where I was pointing but it was just deep enough into the undergrowth that I couldn't see it. She jumped aside and pushed away the vines and branches. Her efforts revealed a plank of solid wood, not from a tree branch, but wood that had been purposefully cut and polished.

"Ah, you see?" Kim burst out with pride. "Dumb luck!"

"No," I said. "Not dumb luck. Those vines are not sticking to that wood. I think if we look around we will find broken twigs and branches nearby and it looks like those branches there have already been moved at least once."

"Someone else has been here?"

"Yeah. Probably from another direction or we would have seen the signs, but someone has definitely been in this spot before us and not long ago." I looked closer at the disheveled leaves. "There's something there."

"Then let's have a look, "Kim said. She reached over to some branches near her. "Shall we?"

I came to her side and grabbed a handful of greenery. We pulled in opposite directions and the vines and leaves fell away to reveal a carved wooden door. At the base of the door were some loose papers.

# Chapter Twenty-Two

## *The Realm of Perfection*

**Pa'kevutu: Kwanchu    Vipya Province**

On the great wooden door was carved the symbol we had seen in the books on the professor's desk: three curved arms with three smaller symbols at the end of each. It was the mark of the Dreamweaver. We had found an ancient temple dedicated to her. It was sunken into the ground and covered with greenery. Fortunately for us, the doors swung inward and we were able to get them open enough for us to crawl through. We made some torches and lit them. I picked up the loose papers from the ground and looked them over.

'What are they?" Kim asked.

"Some ramblings about Kugoya. I think he's talking about our disagreement with your former boss." I read some more. "But he makes it sound like some kind of cosmic revolution." I flipped through the papers. "Here's a poem." Another sheet was torn crinkled. "Who knows what this is!"

"He's losing his mind," Kim muttered.

"Maybe," I said, shoving the papers into my dry kevan pocket. "Or maybe he's just struggling with all those spiritual principles he's trying to grasp."

"If you ask me, he's lost his grip. I mean... why go to such trouble to cover up those branches out there and then foolishly drop his crazy letters in the dirt?"

I looked at our surroundings. "It's some kind of special game to him, I suppose."

"And you're all too happy to play along."

I said nothing.

We stood inside a small corridor. Small shafts of light tried to make it through branches and leaves and the holes in the ceiling ripped from growing roots and branches let in a little more light. We moved our torches from side to side to get a look at the walls but there was nothing to see except rotting wood and broken glass. The corridor led into a great room. There the scene was different. There were pillars and altars broken into pieces and wrapped in the roots and branches of invading trees but still distinguishable. That was not what held our attention, though. One wall was filled from ceiling to floor in drawings and paintings full of curious symbolism. Kim and I held up our torches to study them.

"They look like some of the images we saw in the books," Kim said.

"Definitely Dreamweaver imagery," I said.

"Look here," Kim said as she lifted her torch. "The image of a woman but with extra arms spread out across the sky." Kim looked closer. "Her eyes are closed and there are clouds drifting in and out of her. Another set of arms look like they're playing with something."

"Spinning. She's spinning."

"Is she the Dreamweaver?"

"That would be my guess."

"I thought you knew. I thought maybe you read their book or something."

"The Cult of the Dreamweaver didn't have a main text, just some commentaries and guides," I said. I moved some more vines aside to try and reveal the entire wall..

"How can you have a religion without a book?"

I put together some stone pieces from a broken column to form something I could stand on. I pushed back some leaves and exposed a part of the artwork in the upper corner. When I put my torch near it, the drawing of a strange mystical world was revealed. "See this?" I said.

Kim moved closer and held up her torch.

"Paradise," I said. "The Realm of Perfection. The Cult of the Dreamweaver was not always a cult. It was once the main religion of the people of the islands." I let the flame of my torch move over the images. "They believed that the Dreamweaver created Paradise–a place of Perfection. There everything exists in its most perfect state but when anything comes down to us it is imperfect because it has left Paradise. Their goal was to return to Perfection through coming together but they knew they could never ultimately know Perfection in their lives. Life is an imperfect expression of the perfect life which is possible only in paradise." I turned to face Kim. "You can't write a book about that. Once you try to put into words the wholeness of Perfection you are already fragmenting it into distorted representations."

"How do you know so much about this stuff?"

I turned back to study the artwork. "My mother," I said. "She was a scientist and a skeptic. She always taught us to question everything, every assumption, every motivation. She's the reason I became a Detective. As a big city cop I became skeptical of the Ceorans and the Corps. They managed to create a whole religion around allegiance to them. I wondered how they managed to do that. I did some detective work of my own."

"And?" Kim asked.

"They hijacked the Dreamweaver theology. With no central text to make a claim to its true doctrines they were able to change them over time."

"How?"

"I'm not certain. Maybe through coercion or the development of new myths or a combination of other things. The history is murky, at best, but the effects were crystal clear. The goddess figure was replaced by the Corps themselves. The idea of an unattainable Perfection was replaced by the figure of the perfect worker sought through a lifetime of struggling for the Corp."

Kim looked down. "Awri's father."

"Yeah," I said. "He thought his father died a hero of the Corp until Ishlan told him otherwise. Awri probably dedicated his life to the memory of his father. He wanted to follow in his footsteps.

He joined Savuran and became a Detective." I looked back at Kim. "He must have been devastated at the words that Ishlan spoke. He has been trying to understand his life and his purpose ever since."

Kim stepped back a few paces and looked at the drawings on the wall. "Did Ishlan know about the Dreamweaver?"

"I don't think so."

"Then how did E end up talking like one of her disciples?"

I walked to a lower section of the wall still covered in vines. "I think E just happened to hit upon a similar idea."

"Which was?"

I brought my torch down to a corner of the wall. "Which was that Perfection can be obtained when we rejoin with the unity of all things, when we return to Paradise."

"You mean when we die. The corps already promised that."

"The difference being that there is no need for someone to grant you the privilege. In the eyes of the Dreamweaver we are equally all part of the one dance of life."

I could tell Kim tried to understand what I was telling her. That alone made the moment poignant. I had not known Kim long but she was not someone who pondered deep questions. It was not because she was any less intelligent than anyone else it was just that she preferred action over analysis. Something must have intrigued her, however. She wanted to give this idea some thought.

Kim found a place to anchor her torch then sat herself down on a fallen timber. "So, what's the connection?" she asked.

"Between?"

"What's the connection between Ishlan, the Dreamweaver, and Awri? Why is Awri so interested in a dead religion?"

"He was led here by a vision, remember?"

"Yeah, a vision from a dead guy. He must have just crossed over to the Island of Perfection and decided to send back some sketches." Kim thought for a moment. "You don't really think it was a message from the dead guy do you?"

"Who's to say?" I sat down as well. "Was it a message or was it a trigger?"

"A trigger?"

"The dead man may have triggered a memory in Awri, a memory of the death of Ishlan which may have triggered yet another memory, maybe some long forgotten story about the Dreamweaver. There is one thing that connects what Ishlan said and the Dreamweaver Cult."

"Oh, Exi," sighed Kim. "You always did love your moment of suspense. OK, I'll bite. What's the connection?"

I stood up and pulled back some loose leaves and vines from a lower portion of the wall. When I had the section cleared, I brought my torch up to it. There on the wall just below one of the hands of the Dreamweaver was an image of a great whirling mass of small dots and wisps of white against a dark background.

"The Spiral of Unity," I said. "The Dreamweaver spins the fragments of Perfection into reality. The Shadow-Keepers use a great whirlpool of energy to maintain the gravity and atmosphere of this world. Ishlan saw the great whirlpool of the Shadow-Keepers. It changed eir life and how E thought about the world. It formed eir understanding of life and death. It transformed eir religious ideas of the Pursuit of Perfection. It was what led em to say the things E said when E died, the things Awri heard. It was what triggered a memory of the Dreamweaver."

"And brought him here," Kim added.

"Yes."

Kim stood and grabbed her torch. She walked around the room. "You think he was here, then?"

"Yes. All of these vines and branches along the wall should have been a lot harder to move."

"But not if they had already been moved before we got here." She inspected some fresh cut marks on a branch.

"Right. He tried to cover it all back up before he left but he was definitely here. The papers prove that."

Kim turned to me. "And do you think he found what he was looking for?"

I looked at the drawings on the wall again. "I don't know. I think he may have stood here as we are and got just as confused."

"If he gets any more confused he's going to blow a connection in his head. He's about two steps to the door of the Wacko Ward already."

I giggled at Kim's ability to make any situation the focus of a joke. It was something I hated about her when I had to chase her down as a murder suspect but which I appreciated about her now.

"There's another possibility, though," I said.

"Yeah, what's that?"

"That he stood right here, just as we are now, and saw something we do not. He may have put it all together: the visions of the Dreamweaver, the wisdom of the Shadow-Keepers, and the words of Ishlan. It may have been like putting together the pieces of some great cosmic puzzle until he could see the whole picture. He may have found what he has been seeking."

"And how will we know which Awri he is: philosopher or fanatic?"

I took my torch and walked past Kim toward the corridor and the door from where we came in but before I passed Kim I gave her a look of dissatisfaction. I thought she was being harsh on Awri but that was her way.

She expected a lot from people and rarely did she get what she hoped. It was a curse she put on others because she put it on herself even more. She may not have talked about the Pursuit of Perfection but somehow it had been fused into her bones and the dark side of that pursuit haunted her and clouded her view of others.

"We won't know until we find him," I said, walking away from her.

"And how are we going to do that?" she called back to me.

I didn't answer her. I walked through the doorway, extinguished my torch, and moved into the forest. Would she still want to know the answers? I thought to myself. Or, has she had enough?

I heard a twig snap a short distance behind me and I smiled.

# Chapter Twenty-Three

## Everywhere and Nowhere

Pa'kevutu: The Island Of Kwanchu    Ruez

I wish I could adequately convey to you the charm and grandeur of the town of Posa. It receives the bulk of the visitors to Kwanchu since it lies on the Eastern side of the island and is closest to the Northern end of the Kevutu mainland. It is why Kim and I were there. But I am getting ahead of myself. Let me first tell you how we got there.

After leaving the temple in the Vipya Province, Awri's trail went cold. We followed descriptions of him North as far as the town of Ruez but then he seemed to disappear. We searched the town and asked everyone we saw about him. Those who did see him did not forget him. He made an impression. He was scraggly in appearance and would rant on about new freedom and the glory of Perfection. He attracted attention wherever he went and that was what worried me most. Local agents of Savuran would be on his trail soon as well. He was making it too easy to be found. I wanted to find him first.

It was if he was everywhere and then he was nowhere. The stories stopped as quickly as they began. He was there one day and then he was not. We kept looking and soon we saw the Savuran agents looking for him. We followed them, looked where they looked, dug into places where they hadn't, and searched every rock we could turn over, but he had vanished.

Days later, Kim and I sat in a cafe for some lunch. We were both exhausted and frustrated. The sky was fall of heavy gray clouds that looked like they were ready to fill the sky with snow at any moment. I wasn't used to seeing snow so soon and the cold made me miss the mainland.

Inside, the cafe was rustic but comfortable. Wide and tall wooden beams  supported even greater wooden planks at the top and a warm fire raged to one side. The atmosphere was filled with the smells of hot food and cold ale and the sounds of discussion and laughter.

"How could he just disappear?" Kim said, taking a bite from her sandwich. "It's like he was here and then suddenly he wasn't. No one's seen him."

I stared at my own sandwich but said nothing. I just wanted to close my eyes and go to sleep.

"Do you think something could have happened to him? Do you think maybe he's…"

"I don't know, Kim. I'm tired and out of ideas. I can't even think about it anymore."

Kim stared at me as she chewed. Maybe she was actually worried about me for a moment, I'm not sure, but the tone of her voice softened.

"You know," she said. "He's probably off in the Northern woods someplace contemplating spinning plates of hotcakes and the deep mysteries of a cup of roonberry tea."

"The mystery being: why would anyone actually drink that stuff?" I said.

"I hear it's an acquired taste," Kim said.

I chuckled but said nothing else. I wanted it to look like I was holding my attention on my food.

"You should eat," said Kim. "Who knows how long it may take to find him."

"Maybe it's time we stop looking."

Kim stopped moving. "What? You're giving up. The great Detective Exi is halting the chase? I thought I'd never see the day."

"He clearly doesn't want us to find him," I said. "Maybe it's time we let him go on his way. Besides, it could be that we're not really helping him by looking."

"Let me guess," said Kim, darting her eyes around. "The two

goons in the dark kevans. Far corner. They think they're being inconspicuous but stick out worse than a lighthouse on a sister-less night."

I couldn't help but smile at my own arrogance. Of course Kim saw them too. She had once been an admirable adversary for good reason.

"The closer we get to him, the closer those two get to us," I said, still stirring my food. "Besides, I'm tired and I've been thinking about what you said."

"Go on," said Kim. She reached for her tea and was about to take a sip. "I'll try not to gloat on this rare moment of sagacity."

"Is that your new big word for the day?"

"You're changing the subject," Kim said.

I adjusted my position in the chair. "It pains me to say you may have been right. People need to know what's going to happen if we don't find ways to regulate our impact on this planet. Unchecked population growth and the depletion of resources needed to support that growth will only cause our people great suffering."

"But you are a sign of hope, a Third Child."

"I bring equal helpings of hope and despair but if I can convince others before it is too late, then I can focus on the hope." I drank some ale and thought about what I said. I would first have to convince myself. "I think it's time I go back to Yakrutich."

"OK by me," said Kim. "I've had enough of these small towns and cold beds."

Kim and I finished up our food, left the table, paid our bill, and headed out of the restaurant. As we passed the table of the two Savuran agents trying their best to blend in, Kim jeered out a loud, "Hey there, boys!" She bent down and whispered into the ear of one of them but loud enough that I could still hear her. "If you followed us any closer," she whispered. "I'd have to pull your nose out of my ass!"

She passed them by and I had to snicker.

As we walked out the door, Kim said, "It's getting so that I can't tell the difference between those Savuran snoopers and my old Wesandt buddies."

"I suspect that if your old boss Mag has his way there won't be any difference."

"You think he'll combine the two?"

"I think he doesn't like limitations on his influence."

Kim sighed. "Talk of despair..."

After spending one final night in Ruez we set out for the long road that led east across the island to Posa. It took us a couple of days and several stops to small cafes and inns along the way to get there and the cold winds and occasional snows slowed us down. We said little to one another as we walked. There wasn't much more to say. The chase was over, the target got away. We were tired, frustrated, and ready to head home.

I looked forward to settling in on a passenger ship and sleeping during the whole trip. I wasn't getting any younger and left my youthfulness and the spark of a possible romance back in the big city. This trip had turned out to be a foolish interruption to my life but I knew I would never be able to live with myself if I didn't find out what happened to the man with whom I had worked so closely. I had seen him grow into a fine detective. I had mentored him and trusted him. I couldn't have done anything different.

We entered the gates of Posa and our spirits lifted. As I alluded earlier, Posa is a town of charm and grandeur. It is a tourist destination serving the curious and the restless who sail from the mainland of Kevutu north to the romanticized snow-covered peaks and frozen valleys of eastern Kwanchu. Its streets are lined with pleasant little shops filled with curiosities and amusements. Its cafes compete with each other for the most creative menus and its inns work to fulfill every fantasy of grandiosity. We felt like we had arrived for a long-deserved vacation.

We found a quaint little inn near the docks, booked ourselves passage to Yakrutich for the next morning, then spent the rest of the afternoon walking the streets before the evening meal.

"So," Kim said between the natural rhythm of our footsteps in the snow sprinkled streets. "What you got waiting for you back at home?"

"Yakrutich or Gycron?"

"You were born on Keyevich?"

"Guess that makes me a Western Islander," I said without any pretense of pride.

"But you're going back to Yakrutich?"

"Yup."

"What's keeping you there?"

I glanced over at Kim. "What are you getting at, Kim?"

"C'mon," Kim smiled. "It doesn't take a detective to figure it out. You're no longer at Savuran, you have no children–at least you haven't mentioned any–and what mother doesn't mention their children? You have no other family that I know of... and I would know that." She paused a few steps. "What's calling you back to Yakrutich? Or, should I say... who?"

I looked ahead to see what was down the path. "You really going to do this, Kim? I didn't think you were the gossipy type."

"I'm not planning to take this to my sewing circle over tea and crackers and you're dodging the question again."

We walked further down the road when I noticed a commotion not far ahead. "Looks like there's a marketplace up ahead. I think we should take a look around."

"OK, keep your secrets. Just trying to spice up the walk a little," Kim said.

I sighed. "OK. It's likely we won't see each other after this adventure is over." I lowered my head and looked at the snow glisten in the sunlight. "There is someone. Not sure if it will turn into anything but I'd like to at least see what's there."

"Ahh, young love," Kim said jokingly.

We continued down the path and turned a wide corner into an open space. People had stalls set up to sell their wares. The markets were one of the few places where the Corps allowed people some personal freedom and entrepreneurship. It was a farce, of course. People were allowed to sell things so long as their products were deemed inferior to those of the Corps. The whole enterprise provided the Corps a false image of cooperation while it actually gave them yet another method of control.

Part of the facade of the free space was the presence of hawkers and itinerant philosophers. There were allowed to stand on boxes or small platforms and spout their ideas and philosophies to the market-goers around them. Those whose words fulfilled the Parak doctrine of the Corps were allowed to speak all they wanted, of course, while those who spoke other ideas were carefully monitored, mocked, or sent away.

The marketplace was a barrage of sounds, smells, and moving images that attacked our senses until we could separate them all out and move among them. We looked at the myriad of trinkets for sale as we breathed the smells of different foods and heard the words of shoppers and preachers alike.

"You seek greatness?" cried out a voice between a couple of stalls of food and drinks. "Greatness is not a single individual act but a consistency in replicating small good deeds. This is the life of a true Parak dedicated to the mission of the Corp established by..."

Kim rolled her eyes discreetly in my direction then bent near my ear to whisper, "Some things here should not be swallowed."

I smiled and we meandered through the hodge-podge collection of goods. The volume of noise rose as we ventured further into the crowd. Voices called out the types of products on sale, people called out to their friends, conversation and laughter got louder and the preachers tried harder to get the attention of the passers-by.

"You have forgotten," called another voice trying to rise over the cacophony of sound. "You have forgotten who you really are. In stolen moments of ecstasy you remember, but then you work hard to erase the memory. You are the heart of a flame...:"

"You say your life has no meaning," called out another voice in the other direction. "Yet all that you do has meaning if it brings joy to even one other of your fellow..."

"There are only three conditions to the state of glorious imperfection: impermanence, balance, and interconnectivity. All are the warp and weft of the fabric of wholeness and it is up to each of us as sacred individuals to..." cried out yet another voice off to the Northeast.

"Freedom of mind is no freedom at all," cried yet another voice further to the right of the last. Like the life that is given its true meaning through work so must the mind be focused on the true purpose. Any effort to do otherwise will only lead to…"

"Hang on!" I blurted out to Kim. She reached to get a taste of some local delicacy when I grabbed her arm.

"What is it?" asked Kim. "The food poisoned or something?"

"No, wait!" I said and I closed my eyes to focus. "Sacred individuals," I whispered.

"What are you talking about?" Kim said, grabbing a handful of something.

"No Parak or any other person would openly speak of the worth of an individual." I yanked at Kim and pulled her with me. "Let's go," I said.

"Hey! Where are we going?" she cried out, releasing a handful of nuts into the air.

# Chapter Twenty-Four

## *Of the Same Worth*

Pa'kevutu: The Island Of Kwanchu    Posa

Kim and I ran through the crowds at the marketplace until we arrived at the place where I heard the voice. As we came closer we slowed down so that we wouldn't disturb anyone. There were people gathered around a man who stood talking to them. The man looked disheveled but not squalid. He wore a traveling kevan which you probably know, my dear, is a kevan with a skirt that reaches nearly to the top of the foot and comes in drab colors. They have not been in fashion for some time so I was surprised to see him wear one, yet no one scorned him for it.

The sandy-gray kevan included a hood for protection from the wind and dust and he put it over his head even though the wind was chilly but calm. The hood partially covered his forehead and darkened his eyes. The rest of his face was covered in a thick mustache that curved around his lips and merged into a full and long beard that tapered down to a point at his chest.

"Perfection is not something that can be gained but must be pursued," the man said to the crowd. "It is found in the wholeness, the fullness of the one reality…"

"Exi!" Kim whispered. "Is that?…"

I grabbed her arm and gave her a desperate look that pleaded with her to be silent. I didn't want us to be noticed, most especially by him.

But, I had heard it too.

The voice was different somehow. He spoke more slowly, more confidently than before. The tone was a little lower and deeper than I remembered but the inflections and the basic sound was there. It was Awri.

A voice not far from us rose above the crowd. I ducked my head in case Awri looked our way. Kim saw me and did the same.

"But why pursue Perfection if it cannot be attained. Isn't that futile?" the voice of a curious listener said.

"Do you wish to die?" Awri asked the man.

"No, of course not," the man responded.

"And yet you know that you shall. Why continue to live if you have no hope of sustaining your life?" Awri said. The man did not respond. "Every day you fight a battle you cannot win yet you continue to fight, nonetheless. The end of the journey defines the journey itself but is not what is important." Awri turned to look at the crowd as it continued to gather around him. "The end of life gives life value, meaning, and fullness. Grasp that fullness with all your being even though you know you can never fully seize it. So it is with Perfection. We seek it through wholeness even though we can never be fully whole because the path to the goal provides meaning and value."

"Exi," Kim whispered. "That's definitely him. No one else would dare speak words like that in the open."

"Yes, I know," I said.

"Because Perfection is greater than all of us," continued Awri. "It can be defined by none of us. Its pursuit is your own."

"But does that not lead to anarchy and confusion?" asked another voice from the crowd.

"The path is yours alone," responded Awri. "But the road you use to walk it is not. Together we must build the means to allow each other to pursue perfection. A single flame cannot support itself."

"Aren't we going to go get him?" Kim asked.

"No," I said. Kim gave me a blank look.

"But why must we suffer so on this path?" asked a woman in the growing throng.

"You speak of suffering as if it were a punishment," Awri said to the woman. Because we are part of the separation of the whole we experience constant change. Imperfection must always evolve into yet another form as it seeks the wholeness of Perfection. Suffering is nothing more than the reaction to a change. We cannot prevent the changes but we are in control of our own reactions to those changes. Suffering and joy are the winds of change along the path but we determine how to navigate them. Those winds can blow us back or carry us forward."

"Do you hear what he's saying?" Kim whispered with some strain of concern. "He'll attract the attention of the authorities. They'll trump up some ridiculous charge and then carry him away."

"I don't think so," I said.

I nodded in a direction to the edge of the mass of people. There were a few strangers trying to elbow their way into the center of the crowd but with no luck. They tried to be discrete but the array of strangers around them made the task difficult for them.

"C'mon. Let's go," I said softly. I turned slowly and kept my body low so I would not be noticed. Kim followed me until we were far from the sight of the crowd.

"I don't understand," Kim said. "We came all this way to find out where he was and to bring him back with us."

"I never said that was my goal," I said.

"But?" Kim protested.

"I said I wanted to make sure he would be alright."

"But he's not alright. He's going to be arrested and taken somewhere where he will disappear. He will be accused of blasphemy and treason against the Council. How can that be alright?"

"Didn't you see how the people protect him? They want to hear him speak even if they do not yet believe him," I said.

"They can't protect him. You know that. Eventually they will get him."

"I wouldn't be so sure."

"Why?" Kim asked.

"Take a look for yourself," I said and pointed back in the direction from where we came.

Kim turned her head and saw… nothing. The people were still there but Awri was gone. "What?" she said.

"He is like a spectre, a vision, a dream that dissipates upon waking. He speaks of wonders and the wonders remain, but he does not," I quoted from some obscure historical book I recalled.

Kim turned to me in utter confusion. I put my hands upon her shoulders and looked at her.

"He has found what he was seeking and I am satisfied with my search as well. He will be fine. There is nothing more we can do for him." I looked into her eyes and saw that she was starting to understand. She nodded.

"Let's go home," I said and we left.

I never saw him again but I heard his name mentioned many times. He became a legend and something even more than that. For some he was an inspiration and for others he became a symbol for all that is wrong in the world. The one thing he will never become, however, is forgotten.

I know that he continued to speak wherever and whenever he could and that the religion of the Torans gradually developed from those words. I know that the island of Kwanchu became a hotbed for resistance against the expansion of the control of the Corps and that his words were used in their rallying cries. I know that there were many who loved him and dedicated their own lives to helping others find peace and sacredness in themselves. I know that Wesuran would spend a lot of time and energy on trying to erase his memory and influence.

*My dear granddaughter, as much as the Academy will tell you that Wesuran prides itself on its separation from the rest of the society it claims to protect, it is not so. At some point in your training you will come across his name and you will hear the stories they tell about him. Of all his teachings, his words about the Pursuit of Perfection as an individual privilege are the most dangerous. They have caused some to question their role in a society controlled by the Corps and they have brought others toward a whole new theological understanding of our* world but never have I heard him advocate for the death or suffering of others as a means of changing minds or eliminating dissent. This you should know above all things.

My dearest Zoey, the day we were asked to take care of you and you were brought to us was one of the greatest of our lives. You have shown yourself to be an extraordinary child, one who always seeks to do the right thing. All that we ask is that you continue to be just who you are. Without a doubt you will come to face some tough choices in your life and you may seek the words and guidance of others to help you but I urge you to choose your mentors and counselors wisely. Always be true to your heart.

I do not expect you to become a follower of Awri but I also hope that you do not follow the teachings of any other prophet or Ceoran without close examination of their words and the effect they have on all of us. There is one teaching of Awri's, however, that I do wish you to keep close to your heart though it is not the one for which he is most known. Instead, it is a corollary of that maxim. In short, he claims that since we are all part of one perfect wholeness, we are each worthy of the same dignity and value. This, he says, is true for all beings whether Citran or anan, male or female, young or old, Kevutian or Kwanchurian, or between any other comparison of people. Regardless of what you may think of the person who spoke those words, consider them on their own merit. Let them guide you through the difficult times and comfort you in the gentle times.

Remember my dear that your grandfather and I will always love you wherever you go and whatever you may do. You always make us proud and we know you will continue to do so. You have agreed to help and aid, protect, and defend the people of this world and we shall all be the better because of that decision.

Be well, be safe, and be happy.

# Chapter Twenty-Five

## *May You Rise to Meet Them*

### From The Chronicles Of Enlightenment

*Editor's Note: The following manuscript was found among the few remaining belongings of the Revealer before he disappeared forever from the public eye. Note that it is not presented as a revelation but as a final prayer to the people directly from the Revealer himself.*

May your mind turn toward justice and your heart encircle peace.
May you seek the perfection of your own potential.
May your senses take in the world and know the joy of dancing the Dance of Life.
May you share that joy so that the even the Seven Sisters smile upon you.
And when it is time for the spinning to cease,
May you die well and rise to meet them.
May they kiss you and return you to the shining Torans of Paradise.
May you be released into the stardust and know again
The true perfection of peace and eternal joy.

# The Milleran Cluster

Follow the plight of Exizoyn and her daughters as they resist the power-hungry forces of the Kevutian Conglomerate amidst the planetoids of the asteroid belt known as the Milleran Cluster in this first thrilling four volume science-fiction series.

### Of Eternal Light

An infant child is taken away from the Gycron city hospital on the island of Keyevitch, a strange man heads to the forbidden barrier at the edge of the world, and a detective is murdered within the walls of a local research corp. These are some of the mysteries that Chief Detective Exi and her partner Junior Detective Shorix from the Savuras Security Corp are asked to investigate. In the process of seeking answers they discover the mysteries of the strange ancient people known as the Shadow-Keepers who thwart the technological progress of the people of the planet of Pa'Kevutu, the intractable condition known as the Third Child Syndrome which prevents couples from having more than two children, and the conspiracy of the builders who have profited from using substandard building materials while they disregard the damage and death caused by their disintegrating structures. In the pursuit of answers to the causes of these injustices and their perpetrators, Exi and Shorix discover the truth about the world they live in and the role they each must play to keep it from being exploited to the point of extinction.

### The Forever Horizon

When the erratic but brilliant engineer Ty is nearly torn apart by excavation equipment, it is up to his friend Zoey to rescue him. On board the first explorer sun ship, the Constantia, Ty soon discovers that the failure of the enormous machine was no accident. Meanwhile, on his home planet of Pa'Kevutu, a simple act of defiance turns into a large scale revolution that threatens to change the oppressive corporate governmental structure. Hoping to distract the people from the message of the rebels, the corporate executives send the Constantia on a controversial mission to find much needed resources on a large asteroid. What Commander Wek and his crew discover is that the planet is the home of yet another human race but that fact does not dissuade them from their mission to rape the planet. With only a fleet of small defenseless orbiters and a great deal of determination, the inhabitants of the planet of Pa'Chot decide to defend themselves. The war for the control of the collection of asteroids known as The Milleran Cluster begins.

## The Suicide Fire

Erut is a simple farmer who found himself forced into the military by the power-hungry Kevutians bent on controlling all the asteroids of a region known as the Milleran Cluster. He is shipped to the verdant planet Pa'Myshka only to be falsely accused of stealing from the fees imposed on the subjugated Myshkans. He escapes from his fellow soldiers only to find himself amidst a band of rebels known as the Sifuti.

## The Song Of The Mother

Ony'a and Erut are rescued from the onslaught of the Kevutian forces on the planet of Pa'Myshka by the stranger known as Zao but their troubles are far from over. Ony'a wants to take revenge against the Kevutian forces and the cruel dominion they have built over the other planets of the collection of asteroids known as The Milleran Cluster. Over time they have tortured and imprisoned the inhabitants of those worlds in their never-ending quest for resources and faithful workers of their Corps. Erut has become one of the prisoners and desires his freedom and a chance to destroy the empire known as The Conglomerate. The two will separately battle the domination of The Conglomerate and its heavy-handed ruler Yaveh Yeves III until they meet together to solve an even greater mystery: the previously unknown planet of origin.

# Appendix

## Terminology

**Abrasan**

The Kevutian title for priest. The word is derived from "abrasive" because they consider themselves lowly like dirt but abrasive like grit on sandpaper that works away impurities. Abrasans are often addressed with the honorific 'Kozan.' They either begin their ministry as sacred non-gender people or choose to become non-gender as a physical representation of Perfection.

**Anan**

A non-Citran, a person not connected to a corp or a non-citizen.

**Ceoran**

The executive officer of a corp or corporation

**Corps**

Companies that run the government and the lives of the people. Workers  not only get their employment from the corps but also get their housing and  all the other basic requirements for living.

**Citran**

A citizen or employee of a corp.

**Firans**

People who put out fires

**Kozan**

Title of respect for an abrasan or priest.

**Parakanism**

A religion begun on Pa'Kevutu that emphasizes the Path of Perfection through the guidance of the Corps.

**Shadow-Keepers**

A term for the Watchers who came from the original planet.

**Toranism**

A break-away religion of Parakonism that stresses the individual attainment of perfection and virtue.

**Wesandt**

A security corp on Pa'Kevutu.

# Other Books

**Non-Fiction**

- Spirituality
  - A Different Calling: A Manual for Lay Ministers and Other Non-Professional Facilitators of Any Spiritual Tradition
  - Many Leaves, One Tree: A Collection of Aphorisms Inspired by the Tao Te Ching
  - The Purpose Derived Life: What In The Universe Am I Here For?
  - Three Guidelines for Ethical Living
  - Playing Cards and the Game of Living Well
  - The Emergence of God: The Intersection of Science, Nature, and Spirituality
  - The Langer Deck
  - Emergent Spirituality: Principles and Practices at the Intersection of Science, Nature, and Spirituality
  - Open Hearts and Open Doors: Radical Hospitality in the Church
  - Let Us Wander: A Ministry of Music and Arts
- Games
  - 52 New Card Games (For Those Old Cards)
  - 36 New Dice Games
  - 40 Games for Forty Dice
  - Castle Imbroglio: An Escape Adventure Book
- Music
  - A Guide to the Art of Musical Performance
  - A Theory for All Music

- Book 1: Fundamentals
- Book 2: Chords and Part-Writing
- Book 3: The Tools of Analysis
- Book 4: Parametric Analysis
- Rounds and Canons for Peace and Justice
- Music for Unitarian-Universalist Choirs
- Songs of Worship
- 50 Songs for Meditation

## Fiction

- Science Fiction
  - The Milleran Cluster Series
    - Of Eternal Light
    - The Forever Horizon
    - The Suicide Fire
    - The Song of the Mother
    - The Journey of Awri
- Theater
  - Four Comedies
  - 10 x 10: Ten Ten-Minute Plays Book 1
  - 10 x 10: Ten Ten-Minute Plays Book 2
  - 10 x 10: Ten Ten-Minute Plays Book 3
  - 10 x 10:Ten Ten-Minute Plays Book 4
  - Ageless Wisdom: Multigenerational Plays for Worship
- Poetry
  - Looking At The World: A Collection of Poetry

  - Prayers

# Final Note

Thank you for reading this book!

If you enjoyed reading it please let me know
and please consider writing a positive online review.

Ken Langer

Contact Information
personal website: http://kennethplanger.com
book site: http://brassbellbooks.com
Email: klangerdude@gmail.com

www.ingramcontent.com/pod-product-compliance
Lightning Source LLC
Chambersburg PA
CBHW021120130626
46554CB00002B/785